Beneath the Gypsy Moon

Beneath the Gypsy Moon

by

Darlene Blythe

This is a work of fiction. The names, characters, businesses, places, events, and incidents are used in a fictitious manner. Any resemblance to actual persons, living or dead, or actual events is purely coincidental.

Copyright © 2015 Darlene Blythe
All rights reserved.
Cover art by Pat Morris

ISBN-10: 1519262930
ISBN-13: 978-1519262936

Acknowledgments

I would like to thank Valerie Utton, my editor. Her knowledge, guidance, and expertise have greatly improved this novel.

A special thanks goes to Jim Nilsson, Dan Nilsson, and the entire Nilsson family for their support of Beneath the Gypsy Moon, and my previous novel, The Last Summer Rose. I am very grateful for all their help with merchandising the books.

I would also like to thank retired K-9 police officer and trainer Doug Humphry, Hartford police officer Tom Knapp, and Donna Graham, RN, for sharing their extensive professional knowledge with me.

Also, thank you to my technical advisor Rob Decker, and cover artist Pat Morris.

And a special thanks to you, my readers, for your interest in my novels. Your gracious comments and enthusiasm have made my writing endeavors a very positive and rewarding experience.

Chapter 1

The traveling circus came to town bringing an air of excitement along with its colorful painted wagons. The townspeople gathered under the enormous green and white striped tent that had been set up in the field where the old fairgrounds used to be.

Meghan held onto Rosie's hand, a faint smile tugging at the corners of her mouth when she glanced down and caught the look of wonder in her child's eyes as she watched a man with slick black hair swallow a fiery sword. Rod made his way back to where they were seated carrying a bright red cardboard tray holding tall plastic cups filled with soda, and large red and white bags filled with popcorn.

Together, they watched clowns honk their horns as they rode tiny tricycles around and around in circles. During the next act, Meghan and Rosie felt shivers of fear. Lions, sitting on their pedestals, roared ferociously while pawing at the air. Orange and black tigers jumped through rings of fire. Acrobats swung from high wires, somersaulting down through the air to reach out and catch the swinging bars below them. Elephants carried women dressed in silvery costumes, their trunks held high. Enchanting horses pranced around the outer edge of the ring, carrying men and women in colorful garments.

When the last act was over, the ringmaster, wearing a shiny black coat with tails, a matching top hat, and tall black boots stepped back into the center of the ring. "Don't leave just yet folks!" he bellowed. "The fireworks display is about to begin!"

The crowd cheered and cheered. As their cheering began to die down, sudden deafening booms and brilliant explosions of light and color filled the sky just beyond the huge tent, catching Meghan by surprise.

Rosie pulled free of her mother's hand desperate to catch another glimpse of the horses being led away. Meghan glanced down expecting to see Rosie standing next to her, but she wasn't there. She was... gone.

Meghan froze in shock before turning to look up into Rod's eyes, her face twisted into a mask of horror and pain. Panic rose inside her as she pushed through the crowd wildly—frantically searching for what felt like an eternity. She cried out Rosie's name over and over again, but no one seemed to hear her over the continuous succession of explosions being set off at the end of the fireworks display.

Rod moved hurriedly in a different direction than Meghan to search for his little girl, but he didn't catch sight of her either. Just a few minutes later, while Rod was pushing his way through the now dispersing crowd, desperately searching for a security guard, circus wagons were already beginning to roll down the dusty road away from the old fairgrounds.

In the darkness, Rosie stood transfixed by the gypsy camp. Fireworks were still shooting up and into the night sky, each burst of light illuminating all the fascinating people and animals moving about in the carefree atmosphere. Two men were busy loading lions into a cage that sat atop a wagon, its gaily colored wooden sides carved with sculptures of roaring lions, prancing horses, a giraffe, and monkeys swinging from thick brown vines.

Another man and a woman were loading horses into a small trailer. After they loaded the horses, the man and the woman went over to where the lion trainers were.

Rosie made her way unnoticed to the rear of the trailer. Anxious to see the beautiful horses again, she climbed up onto the back of the trailer. Just as she reached the top, she lost her balance and tumbled down into the horse's living quarters. Frightened, she reached for the top of the ramp to pull herself up again, but it was too high. Hearing voices just outside the trailer, she scooted backward and hid between the loose bales of hay. The two horses, just a few feet in front of her, nodded their heads slowly down at her. She heard the engine start and felt the trailer begin to move, and on the long gently rolling ride down the road that led out of town, she curled up in the pile of hay and fell asleep.

As shadows deepened in the black night, the Search and Rescue Team continued to search every inch of the fairgrounds. But the dry, dusty condition of the ground, and the huge number of circus goers' footprints crisscrossing the fairgrounds, made it impossible for the dogs to pick up the missing girl's scent. As they moved on to enter the adjacent forest, Rod stood answering all of the detective's questions, his hysterical wife being unable to provide them with any rational communication. And sometime between the Search and Rescue Team arriving and Rod carrying her home, the world around Meghan swirled and began to fade away.

After settling Meghan into bed and getting her to take something to help her sleep, Rod returned to the wooded area to join the search for his missing daughter.

The Search and Rescue Team moved slowly through the forest, the darkness and rough terrain making the area hard to cover. Still, they were determined to come out of the forest with a happy ending to the night's sudden and terrifying turn of events. In spite of all of their efforts though, in the early morning hours just before sunrise, the Search and Rescue team led their dogs back to the command vehicle with their eyes lowered and their expressions grim.

As the sun was coming up, two state police helicopters hovered above the old fairgrounds. A few minutes later, they turned and tilted upward to make a more extensive search of the surrounding area. That same morning, when the early edition of the local news aired on TV, anchor woman Trisha Peterson with her too-blond hair and perfectly applied pink lipstick made a plea asking anyone with any information about the missing seven-year-old girl named Rosie to please call the Hartland Police Department or The Missing Children Hotline.

The newscast reached into the homes and hearts of the families in town, and in surrounding towns as well, spawning a wave of volunteers. They began arriving a few minutes after the huge clock in the center of town chimed seven times. As the day wore on, the outpouring of extended support in the form of prayer vigils held in local churches began to spread to churches all across the state, all taking place while Meghan couldn't even find the strength to get out of bed.

Rod, haggard and unshaven after hours of searching, now stood beside their bed, uncertainty darkening his eyes as he agonized over leaving Meghan again to continue the search. But he had to. Night was approaching and his little girl was out there somewhere, lost. She was alone and afraid and he had to find her. Besides, Meghan would soon be asleep again. She had taken the prescription pills he had picked up at the pharmacy and brought to her. As her eyes closed, he turned away and left the room, closing the door quietly behind him. In the kitchen, he emptied the pot of freshly brewed coffee into a thermos and carried it with him as he went out the front door.

Upstairs, Meghan lay in bed curled up in the fetal position. As she settled into a drug induced sleep, long buried memories came alive in her subconscious, shocking scenes being played out in her mind's eye.

"Didn't you hear? There was an explosion late last night... A truck driver was killed... Imagine finding out your fiancé was blown to pieces... They could barely find any remains at all... Just a few bits of bone fragments here and there to bury."

Meghan spent the rest of the night drifting in and out of tormenting nightmares, finally coming awake a few hours after sunrise when Rod returned. She listened to his footsteps, hoping to hear them charge up the stairs, but they didn't.

The phone rang on and off all morning. First, Meghan's mom had called to say she would be coming to stay with them for a while. Then, one by one, the church women called wanting to know if they could stop by to drop off some of the home cooked meals they had prepared for Meghan and Rod. Meghan's cousin Patty had called too. Now,

Laurie was on the phone.

"I'm sorry, Laurie," Rod said. "Meghan's not up to speaking with anyone right now."

"I understand.... I just wanted to tell her... to tell you both... that I'm praying for Rosie's safe return," Laurie said before breaking down into tears. She pressed her hand against her swollen abdomen. The last ultrasound had revealed that she was carrying a baby girl. Once she had regained her composure she continued. "I really wish I could be there for Meghan right now, but... well, I think it might be best for her if I don't come over just yet. She was always there for me when I was trying to adopt Ally; and then again when everything fell through. If there's anything Richie and I can do..."

Rod cleared his throat. "I'm afraid there's nothing anyone can do for us right now, except to pray. We really appreciate that Laurie. And thanks for calling," Rod said before hanging up.

Laurie replaced the receiver on her end and sat down in one of the large overstuffed chairs in her living room, burying her head in her hands, weeping for her friend.

Meghan spent the entire day and night drifting in and out of nightmares. The voices in her head continued to play cruel tricks on her. In one of her dreams, she was walking alone in a cemetery. She had lost track of the time and it was beginning to get dark. A man stepped out from behind the caretaker's building and began chasing her, his dark cape billowing out behind him. She was screaming and trying to catch her breath while running and running as fast as she could, her heart pounding wildly in her chest.

In another dream, two drunken men were standing outside a bar. As she passed by, she heard one of the men say to the other, "Her boyfriend was killed in an accident. He's dead.... He's dead...." The horrible content of her dreams kept changing.

Now she was lying in a hospital bed, cradling her newborn baby girl when a nurse stepped into the room, coming closer and closer, holding out her arms, reaching for her baby. Meghan pulled the baby closer to her breast, but the nurse moved quickly and snatched the baby from her arms. Then she hurried out of the room, the sound of the baby's cries and the nurse's retreating footsteps echoing down the corridor.

"My baby! My baby!" Meghan cried as she jolted herself awake. Her nightgown was soaked with perspiration. She stretched her arm across the bed to feel for Rod, but he wasn't there. She made her way to the bathroom, averting her eyes as she passed by Rosie's slightly ajar bedroom door. There, she peeled off her damp nightgown and stepped into the shower. After she dried herself, she slipped into a clean nightgown, and wandered through the house going from room to room calling for Rod, but he wasn't there.

She made her way down to the kitchen and stepped out the back door into the cool night air. She heard a strange sound coming from somewhere out in the darkness and followed the sound down towards the huge oak tree in the back yard. There he was, sitting in the tire swing, his shoulders hunched forward, great sobs wracking his body.

Meghan hesitated for a moment. She had never seen Rod cry before. Then she went to him and folded him into her arms. He reached out and wrapped his arms around her and they held one another, crying and rocking almost imperceptivity until neither one of them had any tears left. Then, leaning on one another, they made their way back up the hill and into the dark, empty house.

The next morning, Meghan's mom, Colleen

O'Riley, boarded the first flight out of W. Virginia. When her plane landed, Rod was there waiting for her. He carried her suitcases for her and loaded them into the car. They tried to make small talk, but after a few minutes there really wasn't anything more to say. Colleen turned her head to look out the window, watching the scenery pass by while Rod focused his attention on the road in front of him.

After he carried her suitcases into the guest room, Colleen followed him out of the room and busied herself in the kitchen, wanting to make herself useful. She fixed a plate of scrambled eggs and buttered toast with raspberry jam, placed them on a tray alongside a cup of hot tea, and carried it up to her daughter's bedroom.

"Hi Mom," Meghan managed weakly, pulling herself into a sitting position.

Colleen set the tray on top of the nightstand beside Meghan's bed. Then, drawing her daughter into her arms, she smoothed Meghan's hair. "Everything is going to be okay Honey. We just have to believe that. Now please eat something. You have to keep up your strength."

"Oh Mom, it's been so hard," Meghan began through tears.

"I know Honey, but I'm here now, and I'm going to do everything I can to help," she said reassuringly.

"Thanks Mom. Thanks for coming to stay," Meghan answered, trying to manage a smile, but then a faraway look came into her eyes and it was as though she was somewhere else entirely. "One moment she was right beside me..." she said wistfully, and then fell silent.

Colleen sat in the chair beside Meghan's bed, just as she would do in the days ahead between doing things like the laundry, making meals, and fielding phone calls. Sometimes she found herself just sitting there, worry lines creasing her brow, gazing at her daughter while she slept.

As the days wore on, Colleen struggled with her own feelings of guilt and helplessness. She should be able to make everything all right for her daughter. And always, there was the excruciating pain of losing her granddaughter. But she couldn't let herself fully give into her grief right now. She was determined to keep up a brave front for Meghan and Rod. But, lying in the guest room bed at night, the tears she wouldn't allow herself to shed during the day slid silently down her cheeks.

On the day she was supposed to leave, it was

with reluctance that Colleen packed her suitcases and watched as Rod loaded them into the car. At the airport, Rod carried her luggage and walked with her to the security gate. There was a line. Colleen sighed and turned to Rod, hugging him briefly.

"Thanks for everything, Mom," he said.

"Remember Dear, Dad and I are only a phone call away," she said.

The next afternoon, Rod went back to work. He'd used up all the vacation time he had coming and there were still bills to be paid. And in all honesty, he needed to go back to work feeling as though he'd probably go crazy if he didn't.

Chapter 2

The sky was turning pink as the plane landed and taxied to the gate. The grounds crew started unloading the wagons, trailers, and baggage as passengers left the plane and made their way to customs. Once they'd passed through customs, the man and woman went to their trailer and drove away while Rosie remained hidden behind the hay. And the horses, lulled into a nearly hypnotic state by the gentle rocking of the trailer, kept her secret safe. After another long mysterious ride, the trailer finally turned down a long dirt driveway and came to a stop.

The man and woman climbed out of the trailer. While they were leading the horses to the barn, Rosie sprang out from behind the hay. She scrambled to the edge of the trailer and jumped down. Leaning a little too far forward, she fell, landing on the unfamiliar ground, bruising her arms and legs. She managed to get herself up and then ran as fast as she could around the side of the barn, hiding there while the man and woman came out of the barn and closed the trailer gate. When she spied them making their way to the house, she walked alongside the barn until she found a place where one of the boards was missing—a space just wide enough for a seven-year-old child to slip through.

Inside the barn it was cool and dark. And it was quiet except for the occasional sound of a hoof stomping, or the swishing of a horse's tail. Rosie wandered around investigating her new surroundings. Her stomach ached with hunger while she searched for something she could eat. In their stalls, the horses ignored her. They were busy chewing on the remains of the hay scattered on the almost bare floor. Finding nothing that would satisfy the gnawing feeling in her stomach, she began making her way toward the back of the barn.

She heard the barn door open and quickly hid behind a large barrel. She listened as the woman stepped into the barn and began murmuring softly to the horses as she went about filling their water buckets and tossing in leaves of hay. The woman stepped out of the barn and returned a few minutes later with a pail of sweet, crisp apples. She fed the apples to the horses from her hand and patted their thick necks. Then she closed their stall doors and set the pail of apples down beside the grain bin before leaving the barn.

When Rosie was sure the woman was gone, she hurried toward the pail of apples. She reached in and took one of the apples and bit into it, letting the juice run down her chin. She sat quietly on an overturned wooden crate and then heard something coming down the driveway. Watching through a crack in the barn-board, she saw a wagon roll to a stop in front of the barn furthest away from the house. It was the wagon she had seen the night before, the one with all the animals painted on its side. She watched intently as two men began moving the lions—a huge male with a massive mane and a smaller tawny female—out of the wagon.

The man and woman had come out of the house and were on their way to the barn to meet them.

"Ceasar!" The man called. "Be sure to put fresh bedding down for them. And make sure that they have plenty of fresh water!"

Ceasar gave a quick nod and a short wave in the man's direction while he and the other man led the lions into the barn.

"Do not worry, Sergi," the other trainer called over his shoulder. We will take care of them."

Rosie wondered for a moment if all of this was really happening. Perhaps she was asleep and this was just a dream. Perhaps she was going to wake up any moment and be in her own bed, happy that she'd had such an interesting dream, but even happier that she was at home with her mama and daddy.

She stayed hidden in the barn all through the day watching the goings on outside until the light filtering through the spaces between the barn-boards faded into darkness. When she began to feel sleepy, she yawned and stretched and searched for a place to lie down.

Rosie curled up on a pile of hay and slept soundly until the last of her dreams slipped away and the shadows beyond her eyelids brightened, turning pink. She slowly opened her eyes to see pale ribbons of slanted light shining through the cracks in the old barn's walls. She heard footsteps, and then the door cracked open. The dark haired woman she'd seen yesterday entered the barn and began murmuring softly to the horses, but stopped abruptly when her eyes fell upon Rosie. Rosie raised her eyes timidly as she lay on the bed of hay in the flood of morning light. The woman cocked her head to one side.

"Well, what have we here?" she asked. "And where did you come from?" When Rosie didn't answer her, the woman moved closer and reached out to take Rosie's hand, some hidden part of her claiming the child for her own. "Come out into the light so I can get a better look at you," she said while gently pulling Rosie up from the hay and leading her out of the barn where she studied her for a long moment. "What is your name, child?" she asked.

Rosie raised her eyes to meet the woman's, but she was too afraid to speak, the woman's dark eyes probing deep into her own.

But the woman had *the gift*. "Your name is Raisa. In Romanian it means… well… never mind what it means. Your name is Raisa now. Do you understand me?"

Rosie lowered her eyes to the ground without making a sound.

"Well, come with me," the woman said, still holding onto Rosie's hand. She led Rosie up to the house and into the kitchen through the back screen door where Sergi was standing in front of the stove frying links of mititei along with eggs in a cast iron skillet. The aroma of the little sausages made Rosie's mouth water.

Sergi turned around at the sound of the screen door closing. "Who is this?"

"I found her in the barn. She must have been living there while we were away."

Sergi's dark eyebrows slanted into a frown. "Where did she come from?" he asked.

"I don't know. She won't speak. She's too afraid."

Sergi's frown deepened. "Well then, we will have to call the authorities and let them figure it out. She must belong to someone."

"Sergi, no..." the woman began. "Why don't we just keep her here with us? If she ran away, she must have hated where she was living. Look at her. There are bruises on her arms and legs. Maybe she was being abused. Or maybe she came from the orphanage and they weren't looking after her properly. They probably do not even know she is gone. I have heard stories—"

Sergi's temper flared. "Valdoma! We cannot keep her! She is not a lost puppy or a kitten. She must belong to someone. Someone must be looking for her! And we will be leaving again in a few months to perform. What are we going to do? Take her along with us? We could get ourselves into a lot of trouble. No, she must go back to where she belongs!"

Valdoma's eyes smoldered. "The only thing I have ever asked of you, you could not give me! A child!"

Sergi's sudden silence was almost as frightening as his anger. Then his face colored with embarrassment as he turned away. Valdoma's words had been like knives cutting deep into his flesh, driving all the fight out of him.

Rosie shrank behind Valdoma in awe of this woman with the colorful scarf wrapped about her head and flowing past her shoulders. She had murmured so softly to the horses as she stroked their smooth necks one minute, and then argued hotly and fiercely with this equally explosive man the next.

Valdoma was still holding onto Rosie's hand as she turned away from Sergi. "Come," she said as she began to lead Rosie to the back door. "It is time for us to feed the horses," she said as though the matter had been settled.

In the barn, Valdoma worked quietly while Rosie stood by and watched. After the stalls had been mucked out and fresh straw had been laid down, she put fresh hay in their feeders and poured scoopfuls of grain on top. When Valdoma finished filling the water buckets and had closed the stall doors, Rosie followed her back up to the house.

When they had gone inside, Valdoma turned to motion Rosie to follow her, but Rosie was frozen to the spot, staring longingly at the platter of sausages and eggs sitting on the table. Valdoma lifted her chin slightly, realization dawning in her eyes, wondering how long it had been since the child had eaten.

She pointed to one of the chairs. "Sit," she said, and then filled a plate and placed it in front of Rosie.

When Rosie had finished eating, Valdoma motioned to her. "Come," she said, "and I will show you where your room is to be." Valdoma started down the hallway, but turned when Rosie didn't follow her. "What's the matter, child?" she asked. Then she thought for a moment. "Do you understand Roma?" she asked. When Rosie didn't answer her, Valdoma asked her in English. "Do you understand me now?" Rosie slowly nodded her head. "Ah, I see..." Valdoma said, and then repeated her words in English. "Come with me and I will show you where your room is to be."

Rosie blinked back tears as Valdoma led her

down to the end of a narrow hallway and into a small room on the left. A large multicolored tapestry filled most of the wall before her. Large squares the colors of ruby, sapphire, and honey made up the blanket covering the small wooden bed. An ornately carved wooden dresser stood against the wall. Sitting atop the dresser were thick crimson candles standing inside tin holders with quarter moons and stars cut out of their sides.

A faint frown appeared on Rosie's face as she pictured her old room back home. Where was the fluffy pink comforter that covered her bed in the big bedroom? Where was her giant doll house? Where were all her beloved stuffed animals? And where was her mama who used to wait for her to climb into bed and then read her a bedtime story?

Rosie thought of her mother and her clear blue eyes, curly auburn hair, and flowery dresses. Her mother was all soft and warm and tender smiles. And she wanted to ask for her, wanted to ask with everything that was inside her. And she wanted to cry really hard, but she kept it all inside until later that night when she was alone in her room remembering how Sergi and Valdoma had argued, afraid they had been arguing about her. She could hear their angry voices now too, making their way down the hall and filling her ears, making her cry even harder.

"What are we supposed to do with her when we have to leave the country to perform?" Sergi demanded. "We have no passport for her. We cannot just pack her into a crate and load her onto a cargo plane!"

"Just leave everything to me!" Valdoma replied sharply. "We have plenty of time before that is to happen. Do not worry. I will come up with something!"

In the morning, Valdoma called Rosie to come and have her breakfast. When Rosie still hadn't come into the kitchen after several minutes, Valdoma made her way down the hallway and into Rosie's room.

Rosie sat on her bed with tear stains still on her cheeks. She stared vacantly, first from one wall, then to another, not wanting to meet Valdoma's eyes. "I want my mommy," she whispered sadly.

"I am your mama now... your mother." Valdoma said. "And this is your room," she added firmly. "Now, come with me and have something to eat."

Less than a week later, the wagons were lined up

to form a caravan. They would all gather together one last time before the summer was over. Valdoma had spent most of the morning teaching Rosie how to bake the loaves of bread they would be bringing along with them. While the loaves were still warm from the oven, Valdoma wrapped them in tea towels and then she and Rosie carried them out to one of the wagons, placing them beside the wine and musical instruments the men were bringing.

The wheels of the wagons creaked under the weight of their burden as they made their way slowly down the old dirt road through the afternoon and into the waning daylight, finally coming to rest under a canopy of sycamore tree branches. There, in the hidden grove, the hungry travelers shared a simple meal of thick slices of the cheese, and the bread Rosie and Valdoma had brought.

The men had built a fire, and were now playing their musical instruments while the women danced. The children ran freely about, laughing and hiding behind trees, playing made-up games until the moon hung low, round, and pale over the gypsy camp. Now, surrounded by the night, the men sat beside the fire, passing around a jug of Cadarca, a wine so dark that it resembled blood.

Some of the women had gone to the wagons to put their little ones to bed. Valdoma and Rosie had remained outside with Baba. Baba was a tiny woman and very delicate—as though all of her bones were hollow, bird like. She had long dark wavy hair streaked with silver, and high round cheekbones. Large hoop earrings dangled along each side of her face, and she wore rings on all of her fingers. The jeweled sandals she wore peeked out from beneath her long loose skirt as she sat perched on the back of one of the wagons.

Her eyes narrowed slightly when she noticed Rosie tilting her head curiously, looking at the charms dangling from her necklace. For a moment, the old woman's attention drifted and focused on the cluster of trees the horses were resting under as if she could envision things no one else could see. When she turned back, Rosie saw reflections of the campfire flames flickering in Baba's eyes—revealing secrets—rural superstitions that had been hidden there.

And it was then that Baba began spinning her shadowy tales woven from gypsy folklore and recounted local legends of disembodied spirits. While she spoke, complete darkness enveloped the camp, saving for the small circle of light that surrounded them.

Chapter 3

It was almost midnight when Meghan slipped into the bathroom to fill a glass with water and take a pill to help her sleep. When she stepped back into the bedroom, Rod was out of bed, dressed in a pair of jeans, and pulling a T-shirt over his head.

"Rod, where are you going?" she asked anxiously.

Rod's heart sank at the sight of his fragile wife. Before he had time to think, the words were out of his mouth as if they had a will of their own. "The police still haven't turned up anything. Not one piece of information that could lead us to her. I can't just sit around and wait any longer. I'm going to find her Meghan. I promise. I'm going to find her."

Meghan leaned into him, weeping softly, her tears sinking into his T-shirt. He held her tightly, wondering if he was going to be able to keep his promise. When he let go of her, Meghan's eyes widened with concern.

"Be careful Rod," she said in a small voice.

In the forest, there was no real footpath to follow, so Rod picked his way through thick underbrush and young oaks with ragged deer-bitten leaves. He climbed over fallen trees and moved deeper into the forest. The air was moister there, the forest floor a bed of rotted leaves. When the trees began to thin, he moved more freely, following the wide circle of light radiating from the high-powered flashlight he was carrying. He had a few bottles of water and a small first aid kit which he had stuffed into the lightweight knapsack over his shoulder, and a loaded gun. He slowly moved through every inch of the forest that was accessible, calling Rosie's name.

Dressed in her pale pink nightgown, Meghan nervously paced back and forth across the hardwood floor of their bedroom. Rod would be alright out there alone in the dark, wouldn't he? She knew that he knew how to take care of himself. He was used to working alone in the woods at night at the explosives plant. He did it all the time. But this was different, wasn't it? This was not the wooded area he was familiar with.

She continued pacing until the pill she'd taken began to take effect, making her feel woozy and a little wobbly on her feet. She had to lay down now, and climbed into bed quickly slipping into a muddled sleep.

Alone in the woods, Rod couldn't allow himself the luxury of rest. Tormenting questions occupied his thoughts as he moved forward, following the rise and fall of the rocky terrain. Had some depraved monster snatched Rosie away that terrible night amidst all the noise and confusion of the dispersing crowd? Had he dragged her off into the woods, hoping to hide her there until the media coverage of her disappearance died down? Or had Rosie simply lost her way in the dark and wandered off into the forest all by herself?

Then a darker, more agonizing thought took hold of him—was she even still alive? Suddenly a wave of nausea swept over him and he had to stop. He swallowed hard, fighting the urge to give into his fears, and moved forward, willing himself to stay focused on his surroundings. He had to stay alert, the distant howl of a coyote and the rough bark of a fox reminding him that real danger could present itself at any moment.

In the grey pre-dawn light, Rod trudged through another tangle of small trees. Thirsty, he raised the last water bottle to his lips, but it was empty. He tossed it into the open knapsack and wiped the sweat from his brow with the back of his arm. He had no choice but to keep moving forward.

By the time the early grey light had given way to a clear blue sky, he had stepped out of the woods and into a clearing, but the relief that he felt was suddenly replaced by a feeling of dread. In the distance, he noticed a confusion of movement in the sky. There were dozens of huge black wings, crisscrossing and circling, drifting downward. Vultures. They were feeding on something. Rod moved forward reluctantly until he was close enough to see what it was. A white tail deer—or what was left of it. It had been torn apart. A light brown coat of fur still clung to its back, but most of the meat had been stripped away, leaving its entire rib cage and leg bones exposed. Its head lay several feet away, its eyes open and unseeing.

Rod let out a deep sigh and passed by, thankful there was still hope. By now, his legs ached. He was bone tired, his thoughts were getting cloudy, and his vision had become blurry. When he saw the wide brook with its rippling surface glittering in the morning sunlight less than a hundred yards ahead of him, he wondered if it was some sort of mirage. But when he reached its bank a few minutes later and fell to his knees to scoop handfuls of clear thirst-quenching water to his mouth, it was every bit as real and refreshing as any water he had ever tasted. He dipped the empty water bottles into the stream one by one, letting the cold water run into them.

He stood and pulled his boots and socks off. He stuffed the socks into his boots and tied the boots laces together, slinging them over his shoulder as he stepped into the water. He made his way across the stream, feeling the cool, hard stones under his bare feet. He was wading waist deep through the middle of the stream when he spied a timber snake gliding purposefully toward him. It was moving quickly, and as it neared him its mouth opened wide, revealing sharp venomous fangs.

A wave of panic sent a shot of adrenaline coursing through his veins. He pulled his pistol from its holster and fired one shot, then another, and watched as the snake writhed and slowly died, pink trails flowing into the water from its now harmless body. As he continued wading towards the other side of the brook, his heart rate slowly returned to normal, but his gaze never left the water.

When he returned home, Meghan was still upstairs in bed. Not wanting to disturb her, he grabbed a cold can of soda from inside the fridge and settled down in front of the television. When he pressed the button on the remote, the screen came to life and a young, clean-shaven reporter dressed in a dark suit and tie stared back at him.

"Good afternoon and thank you for joining us for this edition of the 12:00 o'clock news," he said. "Bringing you up to date on the missing seven-year-old Hartland girl, Summer Rose Mulligan, or Rosie, the child who has been missing from the old fairgrounds area of Hartland since August 15th. The police, along with Search and Rescue teams and volunteers from surrounding communities, have extended their search beyond the fairgrounds and the local area, but still haven't found any clues as to her whereabouts. They are asking anyone with any information on the missing girl to contact the Hartland Police Headquarters."

When Rosie's picture appeared on the screen, Rod clicked the TV off and got up from the chair. It was as if he suddenly couldn't breathe. He paced back and forth before heading out the back door and into the yard. The tire swing hung from the old oak tree a hundred yards in front of him, mocking him. Without thinking, he grabbed the handle of the ax he kept beside the pile of neatly stacked fire wood and raced to the tree. He reached up and gripped the thick rope connecting the tire to the tree and swung the ax into the rope again and again until it broke free and the tire hit the ground with a firm thud.

Watching him from the bedroom window, Meghan screamed. She ran down the stairs and hurried out the back door. "Rod, what are you doing?!" she cried as she ran to him.

Rod lowered his gaze to the ground. "I'm sorry, Meghan. I just couldn't stand to look at it any longer. I'll put up a new rope, I promise. Just not right now, okay?"

Then, shaking his head from side to side, he strode away, leaving her to stand alone and numb, until she finally turned away and headed back to the house. She went inside and up to their bed to rest. By the time she climbed out of bed and went downstairs to the kitchen, it was nearly dinner time and Rod still hadn't returned home. She gazed out the window, her eyes fixed on the severed thick rope and the big black tire that lay still and useless on the ground.

Memories filtered through her mind like buttery yellow sunlight filtering through the leaves of the old oak tree. Memories of the two of them together, Rosie in her tire swing with Rod pushing her, her little legs held straight out, her toes pointing upward toward the sky as she giggled and squealed with delight. It was one of their favorite things to do together, and it broke Meghan's heart all over again, only this time it wasn't just for herself that she hurt, she hurt for Rod too.

The next morning, Meghan made her way downstairs. In the kitchen, she put the coffee pot on and waited while it brewed. In the quiet of the early morning her thoughts drifted back to the time when she and Rod had first met—memories of the mischievous glint in his eyes as they captured her own from across the room at the hotel dance. Of the confident sway of his shoulders the first time he walked into the diner and took a seat at one of her tables. Of the intoxicating fragrance of his cologne mingling with the scent of his black leather vest as they rode his motorcycle down the highway, her arms wrapped tightly around his waist. And finally, the sound of his voice murmuring, "it's wonderful", while they lay in each other's arms, their lips meeting and everything else in the world melting away.

She sighed as she turned to pour herself a cup of coffee and thought about how she might give anything to be able to go back in time to those early days with Rod again. But those days were gone, and wishing for them wasn't going to bring them back. And besides, going back would mean that Rosie wouldn't be a part of their lives and she didn't want to imagine a life without her.

Instead, she tried to focus on the little bird sitting on the branch of the tree just beyond the kitchen window. It was a beautiful summer day, the kind of day she and Rosie would have spent time together. The love Meghan felt for her daughter ached inside her. And love, she thought to herself, was strong, but the heart that held it was very fragile.

After she had finished her coffee, she wandered out to the back porch. Two fields away there were horses grazing leisurely, standing almost side-by-side. She remembered the times she'd taken Rosie through the back yard and past the stand of tall pines to sit on the grass and watch the horses chewing contentedly in their pasture, their tails swishing. Rosie had loved to watch them—had even asked if she could have one. Meghan had gently explained to her that she was too young, but promised to take her over to the fence to visit the horses in the pasture when she got older.

When she couldn't bear to watch them any longer, Meghan made her way around the house to the front yard and started off down the road with no real destination in mind. She just needed to get away for a while, that was all she knew.

When she had been walking for nearly half an hour, she spied the house of her nearest neighbor. She'd only seen it once before, the day she and Rod had taken a ride out to look at their house when they had first seen it listed for sale in the real estate section of the newspaper. But after buying and moving into the old farm house, she'd never had any reason to travel in this direction as the center of town was in the opposite direction.

When Meghan reached the little grey bungalow, there was a woman standing in the front yard pruning rose bushes. When the woman caught sight of Meghan, she lowered her pruning shears and came to the edge of the yard. Meghan noticed silver strands running through her dark hair, and laugh lines that appeared at the corners of her eyes as she smiled.

The woman stretched out her hand. "Hi, I'm Stevie. Pleased to meet you."

"Hi, I'm Meghan," Meghan said shyly while taking Stevie's hand. She pulled her gaze away from Stevie to admire the cheerful little bungalow with its cranberry colored shutters and front door, and the profusion of rose bushes that practically overtook the yard.

"Well now," Stevie said with obvious delight, "I don't get many visitors out here."

The next day, when Meghan went to see if the mail had been delivered, a bouquet of pale pink, apricot, and ivory roses sat in a clear cobalt blue vase on the porch railing. "Where did these come from?" she wondered aloud. Then after a moment it came to her. They had to be from Stevie. "How thoughtful," she whispered with tears in her eyes.

Not having Stevie's phone number, or even knowing what her last name was so she could look it up, Meghan decided she would walk to her house again to thank her for the roses. She would go after dinner as that was when she felt the loneliest. Rod worked second shift at the dynamite plant, so she ate dinner alone most nights. Visiting Stevie would give her a good reason to get out of the house for a while.

After washing and drying the dinner dishes, Meghan dried her hands and left through the front door. As she started walking towards Stevie's, the sun was just starting to set. As she walked along the road in her sleeveless cotton dress, the sun slowly sank closer the horizon, surrendering up the last of its warm golden glow like a sacrificial peace offering.

When she had almost reached the bungalow, she caught sight of Stevie still busy working in her garden. Her gloved hands were carefully clipping long stemmed flowers with heavy clipping shears, her knees resting on the warm, rich soil.

As Stevie lifted her head, she caught sight of Meghan coming up the road. A faint breeze carrying the hint of wood smoke and sandalwood caught her off guard and she felt it keenly for a moment—the missing of a man. Her eyes followed Meghan, and she thought to herself, "We've both lost so much—we've both lost a part of ourselves."

By the time Meghan had crossed Stevie's yard, Stevie had gathered up all the cut flowers, and stood cradling them in her arms. "Come in and have something cold to drink," she beckoned warmly.

Her garden hat had slipped down over the side of her face to cover one of her eyes. As she nudged the hat partially up again, she appeared quirky and endearing and Meghan found herself smiling as she followed Stevie inside.

After filling a large glass vase with the flowers she'd brought in, Stevie poured iced tea into two tall glasses and motioned with one arm for Meghan to follow her into the sitting room. The small room was comfortable, with shelves lining two walls. They were filled with books, bric-a-brac, small green plants in an array of pots, and an ivory bird cage that was home to two faux snow white doves. In one corner of the room sat an old Victrola.

From where she sat in the soft, cushiony armchair, Meghan studied the framed picture of a man that hung on the wall over the small fireplace mantel. He had short brown hair, and grey eyes that complemented his ruggedly handsome face.

Stevie followed Meghan's gaze. "That's Myles," she said, pausing a moment before going on. "He's my husband," she said, a certain wistfulness filling her eyes. "He loves to go hunting and fishing... you know, camping out and all that. He's a real outdoorsman. Sometimes he goes to the betting track. He loves playing the horses." A shadow passed over her features, then she went on as though she felt compelled to explain. "He's away right now. He's been gone for quite some time actually, but I'm sure he'll be back again someday."

Meghan lowered her eyes and nodded slowly, not wanting to pry.

Then, just as quickly as Stevie's expression had dimmed, it brightened again. "Would you like some more iced tea?" She asked.

By the end of what had turned out to be a very warm September, Meghan had been spending a few afternoons each week at her new friend's house. The charming old-fashioned place with its rambling roses, riotous climbing vines trailing over the antiquated white picket fence, and the slightly hidden herb garden was an interesting mixture of the mysterious and the mystical. She found she needed the half-hour walk to Stevie's little bungalow too. It helped clear the cobwebs from her mind.

Today on her way to Stevie's house, it started raining and the cool water felt refreshing. When she came to the edge of Stevie's property, she saw Stevie from a distance, dancing joyously in the rain, in the middle of her herb garden.

Meghan wore a quizzical expression as she approached the older woman who, in her long colorful skirt and ivory peasant blouse, was obviously a free spirit. Not knowing what to make of Stevie's unusual behavior, Meghan asked, "Why are you dancing in the rain?"

She wondered if it was some ancient tribal dance or just one of Stevie's sudden whims. But Stevie just looked up to the sky and laughed. It was just Stevie being Stevie, Meghan decided as she followed her friend through the back porch door and into the kitchen.

Meghan sat comfortably at the kitchen table while Stevie poured two tall glasses of lemonade. The walls of the kitchen were painted a bright yellow, and there were several woven multi-colored scatter rugs placed here and there on the bare wood floor. Clay pots of herbs and flowers lined every inch of the narrow window sills.

The ice cold lemonade Stevie served had just the right amount of sweetness and mint. When Meghan exclaimed how flavorful it was, Stevie revealed that she had just picked the mint from her garden.

Stevie kept the pleasant conversation going while

they sipped their lemonade, elaborating on the different types of herbs she grew in her garden and in the pots on the window sills. She pointed to the ones in plain sight as she spoke of them, explaining their uses in various dishes and different types of beverages.

She was a wealth of information on the healing properties of many different types of herbs and flowers, and Meghan found all the knowledge Stevie shared very interesting. Before she knew it, the remainder of the afternoon had passed and the dark clouds that had filled the sky were beginning to brighten. When the rain had finally stopped, a small spider's web just outside the kitchen window became a prism of color as the sun began to shine again. Meghan and Stevie discovered the source of its colors at the same time—a magnificent arch that spread from one end of the sky to the other.

"Oh look!" Stevie exclaimed. "A rainbow! It's a sign, you know. It's always a sign that something good is about to happen."

And sitting inside Stevie's small kitchen, reflecting on her words, Meghan found herself wishing she could somehow believe it.

Chapter 4

October was amazing—brilliant sunshine and trees bursting with crimson and gold leaves. Laurie was filled with her own glory, her body ripe with the fruit of her womb. The new life inside her was ready to emerge into a world filled with vibrant color.

She was two days past her due date, and the contractions had started late that morning. They were coming nearly twenty minutes apart by mid-afternoon when she called her doctor to let him know she was in labor. Then she had called Richie. She had just hung up the phone with him, and now all she had to do was wait for him to arrive home so he could drive her to the hospital. He had sounded so excited, and in a little bit of a panic, so she had told him not to hurry as they still had plenty of time to make it to the hospital before the baby arrived.

The baby! Excitement flooded her heart. She cradled her belly knowing that she would soon be holding her newborn baby girl, all sweet and pink and velvety soft, in her arms. Then her emotions clouded over with sadness. She had wanted to share the joy of her pregnancy with her friend Meghan so much. But she had to push those feelings away right now. She believed that babies—even babies still in the womb—could pick up on the things their mothers were feeling, and had decided it was her maternal responsibility to bring her baby into the world surrounded by a spirit of love and joy.

She sat down in the rocking chair, her eyes falling on the overnight bag and diaper bag waiting by the front door, reflecting with tenderness on another little baby girl that had been hers a long time ago—a time before she and Richie had been married; a time when she had been working as a waitress at the diner and had still been involved with her ex-husband Joe. She still remembered Richie's words to her back then when everything had fallen apart.

"I just wanted to tell you how sorry I am about the way things turned out with the whole adoption thing. And I just want you to know that I'm always here for you whenever you need someone to talk to."

He had been there for her when she needed him most, and now he would always be there. She was happy now, unbelievably happy with twelve-year-old twin boys, a loving husband, and a new baby girl to welcome into their family.

Next, she called her mom to let her know that the baby was coming. Just as she was hanging up, Richie came rushing through the front door, almost completely out of breath. She laughed when she saw the color of his flushed face. "Calm down, Richie," she soothed. "I just called my mom. She's going to meet us at the hospital. I couldn't reach Pammy though. She was in a meeting, so my mom said she'll call her from the hospital if I'm not feeling up to it."

Funny how things had changed, Laurie thought to herself. Her sister used to be a stay at home mom while Laurie had been the one working outside the home.

Richie nodded his head. "Okay," he said. "Now, let's get you into the car." He picked up the bags by the front door and then rushed to hold the door open for her.

When she stepped outside, she was surprised to see that he had left the car running. "Richie... really," she said.

He turned and gave her a serious look. "Remember how fast the twins came? We barely had enough time to make it to the hospital."

Laurie began to laugh again, but stopped short when she was hit with another contraction. When the contraction was over, Richie helped her into the car, and then climbed into the driver's seat. As they backed out of the driveway and started down the road, Laurie gazed out the window and admired the way the sunlight sparkled on the ruby and gold leaves on the trees. It was as if nature itself was celebrating along with her.

"Remember to stop by the school when we reach Oak Street so we can pick the boys up and bring them along with us," she said dreamily as her mind wandered down a trail of happy thoughts until it was suddenly interrupted by the discomfort of another strong contraction.

Richie's knuckles turned white as he gripped the steering wheel and pressed down a little harder on the gas pedal. He turned his head toward her, his expression registering concern at the sound of her sudden sharp intake of breath. He didn't see the light turn red, but he saw the look of terror on Laurie's face and heard her scream just before he felt the sudden violent impact of the other car slamming into them, and then everything went black.

At St. Joseph's Hospital, Dee and John, Laurie's mom and dad, sat in the visitor's room on the maternity floor, excitedly waiting for Laurie and Richie to arrive.

"I'll be right back Dee," John said before leaving the visitor's room to take the elevator down to the main lobby. Then he made his way out of the main entrance of the building and out to the visitor's parking lot where his car was parked. He gathered up the rest of the gift-wrapped packages from the trunk of the car, neatly stacking them on the floor beside Dee's chair when he returned. "You left this in the car too," he said, pulling her cell phone out of his shirt pocket. "I thought you might want to have it with you."

Dee smiled at her husband of 42 years. "Thank you, Honey," she said, absently taking the cell phone from him and dropping it into her purse. Her eyes drifted back to the empty hallway. "Laurie and Rich should be here soon."

John picked up the newspaper lying on the table in front of him, settled into the chair next to Dee's, and began to read. Dee studied the framed artwork that hung on the wall. Then she studied the flower print on the wallpaper. Then she searched the hallway again for any sign of Laurie and Richie. Finally, she pulled her cell phone from her purse, needing something to do while she waited anxiously.

"Why don't I call Pammy now," she said. "Maybe she's on her lunch break and I can ask her if she can leave work early to meet us here." But as she held the phone up to place the call, she noticed that there was a message in her voice mail. The number on the caller ID was Laurie's, so she pressed the voicemail button and held the phone to her ear, but she didn't hear Laurie's voice. She heard voices—unfamiliar voices in the background.

Dee's eyebrows narrowed in confusion. She pressed the phone tight against her ear and listened closely. The voices sounded like police officers and EMTs at the scene of an accident.

"I can't tell how badly he's hurt or where the bleeding's coming from yet. There's blood all over his face..."

"She's in labor. We're going to have to get her out of the car and into the ambulance right away. She's starting to push—"

"He's unconscious, get two stretchers over here."

Now Dee could hear Laurie crying and she realized the horrible truth. Laurie's phone must have been bumped shortly after an accident, causing it to redial Dee's number. Tears welled in Dee's eyes as she handed the phone to John. Just after he finished listening to the message, the sound of the ambulance sirens filled the hospital parking lot.

John's jaw clenched. "We better get down to the ER," he said soberly.

By the time Dee and John had reached the ER, Laurie and Richie had already been wheeled in.

"Mom!" Laurie whimpered pitifully. "They took the baby!"

Dee's heart lurched. "What do you mean, Honey? Where did they take her?" she asked, fearful of the answer.

"I don't know," Laurie answered, beginning to cry. "Richie!" she called through her tears, but they had already started wheeling his stretcher away.

John turned to Dee. "I'll find out what's going on," he said. "You stay with Laurie."

At the admissions desk, John was asked to answer a few brief questions before the clerk informed him that he would be able to speak with the attending physician as soon as he had finished examining Richie. Then she told him that there was some paperwork to fill out before Laurie could be admitted to the maternity ward.

"What about the baby?" he asked. "Where is she?"

"They took her down that hall to the pediatric room…" the woman started, turning her head to indicate the direction in which they had gone. "They need to—" But before she could finish, John was already hurrying down the hall in the direction she'd indicated.

When he returned to the ER, he found Dee, but no Laurie. "Where's Laurie?"

"They took her into a room to make sure she's okay. We can go in, I was just waiting for you."

As soon as they were with Laurie, John filled them in on what he had found out. "Everything's fine. The baby is fine. They took her to the pediatric room so they could evaluate her. Now they're on their way up to the maternity floor with her," he said. "She's beautiful, by the way."

Dee breathed a sigh of relief. A nurse approached them and gently took Laurie's hand. "We need to make sure you're okay. As soon as we're done with that, we'll bring you upstairs and settle you into a room with your beautiful baby girl. Okay?"

Laurie nodded to the nurse, but there were tears in her eyes when she looked back to her parents.

Dee reached out to hold her daughter's hand. "It's okay Honey. We'll be waiting just outside the room until they're finished examining you, and then we'll go upstairs with you."

"Richie..." Laurie began, but she couldn't find any more words.

"Don't worry Honey," John said reassuringly. "The doctor is with Richie. I'm sure he'll fill us in on his condition as soon as he has finished running some tests."

"Tests? What kind of tests?" Laurie asked, her eyes filling with fear.

John stole a glance at Dee. "They're just routine tests Honey. Just try to relax, okay?"

The nurse began wheeling Laurie toward Obstetrics with Dee and John following behind. While they were waiting for Laurie's examination to be completed, Dee pulled her cell phone from her purse.

"I'm going to try Pammy again," she said. "I'll ask her to pick Ethan and Eric up from school and bring them here so we can all be together." She paused for a moment before going on. "John, what did you find out about Richie? I could tell you were holding something back. Is he okay?"

"He's unconscious," John said shaking his head. "That's all I know."

Dr. Reynolds, the trauma specialist, knocked lightly on Laurie's hospital room door before entering. The soft spoken man with dark hair graying at the temples introduced himself as he moved to the side of Laurie's bed, grasping her hand briefly. He turned and nodded politely to Dee and John, before turning back to Laurie.

"I've just finished examining your husband, Mrs. Carlson. We ran a CAT scan and he appears to have no other injuries other than the trauma to his brain. The cuts on his head were superficial and the bleeding has stopped. The good news is that he's stabilized and breathing on his own. We haven't seen any swelling of the brain and there's nothing to indicate that there is any injury to the nerves. But there is some abnormal brain activity which is a concern to us at this time. He's been moved into Intensive Care where he will be monitored for the next 24 to 48 hours. Our hope is that he will have regained consciousness by then, but if he hasn't, he will be moved into a step-down unit which is located on the same floor as the ICU. If he goes there, Dr. Hastings, a neurosurgeon, will order an EEG and a MRI.

"When a patient is unconscious for a long time, it can lead to memory loss and shortened attention span. Of course, it's too soon to predict anything, but I wanted to make you aware of the possible problems we could be facing at some point down the road. But at this point, let's just take it one day at a time and focus on the fact that he's stable, and that we have good reasons to believe he will make a full recovery. Do you have any questions I can answer for you?"

Laurie glanced briefly at her baby, wrapped snugly in a pink blanket and sleeping in Dee's arms before she returned her attention to Dr. Reynolds. She cleared her throat and asked feebly, "Do you think he'll wake up? What are his chances?"

Dr. Reynolds smiled compassionately. "I cannot say when he'll wake up. There's just no way for us to predict the future. We will just have to wait and see, but we'll keep you updated on his condition. And you should know that I have an enormous amount of confidence in Dr. Hastings. He's one of the top neurologists in the state. I hope you can find some comfort in knowing that your husband is in very good hands." The heavy silence that followed his words let Dr. Reynolds know that at least for now, there would be no more questions.

As he was leaving the room, Laurie turned over onto her side, tears slipping silently down her cheeks. One floor above her, in the Intensive Care Unit, Richie lay so still, that if it wasn't for the slight rise and fall of his chest, and the machines beside his bed monitoring his vital signs, anyone entering the room might wonder if he was still alive.

Chapter 5

In the evening, sitting beside the fireplace, flames cast curious shadows in the semi-darkness. As Valdoma rotated her glass of palinca, it appeared that smoke swirled up from the glass, revealing its true nature—a strange concoction—a witches' brew.

"On our next tour," Valdoma said, "I will ride Bashalde and you will ride Arielle. We will train Raisa to ride Magic. She seems to have taken a great liking to him."

Sergi did not respond right away. He had become accustomed to having Rosie in their home. Now, in the flickering firelight, he pondered Valdoma's words, remembering how Rosie had stood at the pasture gate that afternoon thoroughly mesmerized by the exceptional animal.

And indeed, Rosie had been completely taken by the unusual horse—for he had a wild beauty. He was the color of blue smoke. His coal black mane and tail gleamed in the sunlight. And his eyes—his eyes shone like huge black pearls that seemed to hold the timeless mysteries and wisdom that only belonged to majestic creatures truly at one with the earth, the wind, and the sky.

She watched him turn his powerful body to gallop away, his hooves pounding the green grass of the field. He became smaller and smaller until he was nothing more than a fading blue mist almost completely disappearing against the early autumn sky. And it was right then that she realized that one day Magic was going to carry her away, all the way back to where she belonged.

Finally, after giving Valdoma's words considerable thought, Sergi spoke. "We will begin to teach Raisa to ride him tomorrow. She is not too young to learn."

The next morning, Sergi, Valdoma, and Rosie stood just inside the fence rail.

"Today you are going to learn to ride Magic," Sergi announced. "What do you think of that?" Rosie looked up at him without answering. He searched her eyes, but saw no trace of fear in them. He nodded, and left her for a moment to get a large crate for her to stand on so she could climb up onto Magic's back, but even with the crate, she was still too small to reach so he lifted her up and into the saddle.

He led her around the ring, first at a walk and then at a trot, so she could get the feel of the horse moving beneath her. He showed her how to hold the reins, and let her take them when she was comfortable enough to ride Magic on her own. He stepped back to stand beside Valdoma, and together, they watched as Rosie walked Magic around the inside of the ring.

Sergi laughed out loud. "She is a natural!" he said triumphantly.

From that moment on Rosie practiced every day, working hard at doing everything just the way Sergi and Valdoma had taught her even after she'd grown bored with just riding Magic around and around the ring. Then, on one fine crisp early afternoon before her lesson was to begin, Sergi lunged Magic outside the ring while she and Valdoma watched the horse canter in a wide circle, his hooves soundlessly hitting the ground. When he had finished exercising Magic, Sergi led him over to where they stood and released the long rope from his halter.

Rosie climbed up onto the fence rail, and grasping his thick black mane with one hand, slid easily onto Magic's bare back. She moved the horse away from the rail and into a short trot before he went into a canter and then a full gallop across the open field with Rosie holding on tightly feeling as though she was flying.

This was the first time she was riding Magic without a saddle beneath her. She felt the wind in her face, nearly taking her breath away. She *was* flying! And she was free! Now she and Magic were as one—one with the earth, the wind, and the sky. And she didn't want this exhilarating feeling to ever end. She tangled her fingers tightly into his mane and leaned slightly forward, willing him to go even faster.

She shivered with excitement as he surged forward with even greater strength and speed. When they reached the end of the field, she spun Magic around and he galloped back through the field heading toward the fence where Sergi and Valdoma stood waiting. Magic's powerful muscles rippled against her legs, his coat now slick with sweat. She gently pulled on the reins, slowing him to a canter, and after a while she reined him in again, this time to a slow trot. By the time they were nearly back to the fence, Rosie and Magic were both enjoying a leisurely walk.

"She's an excellent rider," Valdoma said.

"Her lessons have been going quite well," Sergi added, sounding pleased.

"Tomorrow I will begin to instruct her on training a horse," Valdoma mused aloud. "She is very bright, and works very well around the horses."

Sergi nodded his head in agreement.

The next day, Rosie's heart fluttered in anticipation of her first lesson in training a horse. She followed Valdoma, who was leading Bashalde into the ring. In the center of the ring there was a low platform. Standing just inside the ring with Bashalde between them, Valdoma began her instruction.

"First, we must ask Bashalde to do something we know he is ready to do. Otherwise we will destroy his trust. We must also make it easy and pleasant for him to do what we ask, and we must show him that it is better for him to stay in the ring with us.

"Horses are very good at reading body language and this is very important for you to remember if you are going to train a circus horse. You must spend so much time with him that you begin to know what he is thinking and he begins to know what you are thinking. It's also very important to give lots of praise when he has done what you have asked. Always use soothing words and gentle rubs as a reward. So now... go ahead and lead Bashalde to the center of the ring and ask him to step up onto the platform. Remember to praise him if he does what you have asked of him."

Valdoma leaned against the inside of the fence rail and watched as Rosie led the dun gelding to the center of the ring, speaking softly to him. Then she gently coaxed him up onto the platform and reached up to pat his smooth neck. Valdoma applauded lightly and watched as Rosie led him down from the platform.

"Wonderful," Valdoma called out. "Now we will work on a few more of the basic training exercises."

In the weeks that followed, Rosie's days were filled with excitement as she began to learn all the secrets of training a circus horse.

Chapter 6

At St. Joseph Hospital, Laurie, Dee and John were gathered in the family room waiting for their meeting with the neurosurgeon, all of them anxious to find out the results of the EEG and the MRI. A tall slender doctor with short blond hair and honest blue eyes stepped into the room. He had an air of confidence about him as he spoke.

"Hello. I'm Dr. Hastings, the physician who's been attending Richie."

Laurie glanced nervously at Dee.

"We have the results of the EEG and the MRI. The positive side of this is that both tests show activity in the brain. But at this point, the outcome is still undetermined."

John turned toward Laurie. "That's good news, Honey," he said.

When Laurie didn't answer him, Dee piped up. "Daddy's right Laurie," she said, sounding as though she was trying too hard to be cheerful.

But Laurie wasn't fooled as to the gravity of the situation. Richie was still unconscious, and it was day number three.

When Dee arrived at the hospital the next morning, she caught Laurie's doctor at the nurse's station. "How's Laurie doing today?" she asked.

"To be honest, we have some serious concerns. Both Laurie and the baby were supposed to be released today, but Laurie's still not showing any interest in nursing Elizabeth. In fact, she's not showing much of an interest in her baby at all. Before she can go home we need to know she's going to be monitored closely to make sure she's capable of interacting with and caring for Elizabeth.

"We understand she's gone through a lot of trauma, but her coping skills don't seem to be kicking in. Dr. Matthews, the hospital psychologist, will be coming in later this morning to evaluate her. She may want to prescribe an anti-depressant for Laurie for right now. But our concern is for Elizabeth. We can't risk the possibility of anything happening to her or Laurie."

"Oh…" Dee said softly as her gaze focused on nothing in particular. "She was so excited about having this baby. She waited such a long time to get pregnant again. I just can't believe all this is happening..." Her voice trailed off as tears filled her eyes.

The doctor's eyes were filled with sympathy as he placed a reassuring hand on Dee's shoulder.

It was nearly noon when Dr. Matthews, a tall psychologist with dark hair and golden brown eyes stepped out of Laurie's room, pulling the door almost completely closed behind her. She smiled briefly at Dee and John.

"How's Laurie doing?" Dee asked Dr. Matthews before she could continue walking down the hall.

"I'm sure you understand that I'm not able to share anything with you about my evaluation of Laurie's mental and emotional state. Everything my patients share with me is confidential. My suggestion is to talk to Laurie and let her decide how much of what we discussed she wants to share with you.

"What I can say is that there are decisions that have to be made before Elizabeth leaves the hospital. And I'm sure Laurie could use your support in helping her make the right choices for herself and her baby. I'll stop in again tomorrow to see how she's doing, and to see if she has come to any decisions." Dr. Matthews smiled at them kindly. "We're all here to help her all that we can."

"Thank you, doctor," John said quietly.

Dee nodded, but didn't wait for the doctor to walk away before she gently pushed the door to Laurie's room open and stepped inside with John following a few steps behind her. Inside the room, Laurie was lying in her bed, staring blankly up at the ceiling. Her lunch tray had been pushed away from the side of the bed, the entire meal left completely untouched. Elizabeth was sleeping peacefully in the hospital bassinet, dressed in a pink sleeper and covered with a white blanket.

John seated himself in one of the two chairs across from Laurie's bed and sat quietly, his hands folded in his lap. He looked at his wife and daughter, but didn't say anything. Dee had always been better at handling this type of situation—"women's talk"—as he called it. But he was here. He would always be there for his daughter, and he wanted her to know it.

Dee glanced over at the beautiful baby girl, but resisted the urge to go over and pick her up. Instead, she sat on the edge of Laurie's bed. "How are you feeling, Honey?" she asked. Laurie didn't answer, so she continued. "We just spoke with Dr. Matthews, but she didn't share anything with us about what the two of you discussed. We just want you to know that Daddy and I are here to help you any way we can. So please tell us if there's anything you and Dr. Matthews talked about that we can help you with."

A single unshed tear filled the corner of Laurie's eye. "She said she's not comfortable with the idea of sending my baby home with me. She said she's concerned that I'm unequipped to take care of her right now, and that I should consider where the best place would be for Elizabeth right now. She said Elizabeth will be ready to be discharged from the hospital tomorrow morning, and that some kind of arrangements need to be made to care for her."

Laurie's voice thickened. "Temporarily... of course. She's on her way back to her office to write out a prescription for an antidepressant for me, and she's going to set up an appointment with a therapist so I can have weekly counseling sessions. She said that from the hospital staff's observations... and her own *professional* observations, I'm too mentally and emotionally overwhelmed to care for my own infant at this time. And then she said that one possible option is for the baby to go into foster care!"

Laurie's eyes desperately searched her mother's. "Oh mom... it's happening again! This isn't the way it was supposed to be!" she cried as her face crumpled, and she began trembling uncontrollably.

Dee reached for her daughter and wrapped her arms tightly around her, her own heart breaking at the sound of the anguish and despair in her daughter's voice. "Oh Laurie Honey, don't worry. We're not going to let anyone take Elizabeth away from us. We're her family. I can come and stay with you to help out with Elizabeth and the twins for as long as you need me to," Dee said before letting go of her.

Laurie's expression relaxed a little, and she began to gain back some composure. "But what about Richie?" she asked, her gaze once more meeting her mother's. "I don't want to go home without him."

"We'll just have to take it one day at a time for right now, Honey. His condition doesn't seem to be getting any worse, and it could improve at any moment. We'll visit him as often as we can. Hopefully, the sound of our voices will help bring him around. I've heard of that happening before," Dee offered with a small smile. "And we'll get regular reports from the doctors to find out if there's been any improvement," she added, hoping her words would bring some comfort to her daughter, but the expression on Laurie's face remained closed.

Two days later, Laurie was home, in the kitchen talking to her sister Pammy on the phone. "I just left there about an hour ago. They moved him out of ICU today, but there still hasn't been any change in his condition. Dr. Hastings told me he ordered another EEG and an MRI, and that he will let me know what the test results show just as soon as he gets them."

Dee could hear Laurie's side of the conversation from the living room. Elizabeth had fallen asleep in her arms, so she carried her over to the portable crib to put her down for a nap. After a short pause, she heard Laurie continue.

"Thank you for offering Pammy, but Mom's here with me and I don't need anything right now—except to have my husband back here and by my side where he belongs... I just want Richie to come home," she said, her last words choked with emotion.

Dee gazed down at the sleeping baby and sighed. She stepped into the kitchen just as Laurie was placing the phone back into its receiver. She felt completely useless, but she had to do something, so she did the only thing that she could think of. "Laurie Dear, would you like me to make you a sandwich?" She asked hopefully.

"No thanks Mom," Laurie said, blinking back tears. "I think I'll just go and lie down for a while. I'm really tired."

She turned away and walked down the hallway towards her bedroom. When she had turned into her room, it was Dee's turn to cry.

Chapter 7

It was Sunday morning. Rod would have loved to sleep in, but after waking up more than once during the night to the sound of Meghan crying in her sleep, he climbed out of bed and went downstairs to put the coffee on. Then he made his way back upstairs to the bathroom for a quick shower and a shave.

A short while later he was standing at the foot of their bed partially dressed in a white undershirt and dark dress pants, gazing down at his wife. "Come on Meghan," he said. "It will do us both good." It had been several weeks since they had gone to church—the First Baptist Church they had both decided on attending when they had moved into town.

Meghan rolled over beneath the thick blanket and looked up into his eyes. He smiled down at her. Meghan fixed her eyes on his. Her emotions were still so raw and so close to the surface, but he stood there—her six foot tower of support—holding her gaze with unwavering confidence and reassurance.

Finally, Meghan pulled herself out of bed and made her way to the bathroom for a shower.

Rod paused at the foot of the bed for a moment, listening for the steady spray of the shower before putting his dress shirt on, thankful for small victories. Actually he thought, it wasn't such a small victory.

It was a quiet ride down the back roads to the picturesque white church nestled right in the center of town, just a short walk from the post office and the public library. Organ music was playing as Meghan walked through the sanctuary doors just ahead of Rod, stepping into the last row of pews. She didn't want to be the focus of anyone's attention, or feel the stares of sympathy and pity.

As it was, people stole curious glances at every opportunity like when the collection plate was being passed around, or when one person after another rose to their feet to share an uplifting testimony of God's miraculous power in their life. Even when Pastor Earl asked the congregation if there were any special prayer requests for that morning.

Meghan had kept her head bowed for most of the service, staring at the intricate pattern of the muted colors in the sanctuary's carpet. She continued to keep her head bowed when the entire congregation stood and lifted their voices in worshipful song, tears slipping silently down her cheeks. Rod gently placed his arm around her shoulder, offering what little comfort he could.

On the way home, Rod suggested they stop somewhere to have lunch, but Meghan shook her head from side to side. Instead, he pulled into the town grocery store parking lot and asked her to go inside with him to help him pick up things he could take to work the upcoming week. When she stepped into the entryway, her eyes fell on an old circus poster that someone had forgotten to take down and felt a stab of pain inside her as she averted her eyes and entered the store.

They went through the motions of a normal shopping trip, but Meghan doubted she would ever feel normal again. They gathered a few items, and waited quietly at the register while the cashier rang up and bagged sliced meats, three kinds of sliced cheese, fresh produce, and a couple loaves of bread.

When they pulled into their driveway, Rod carried the groceries into the house. Meghan followed, lifting her eyes up to take in the full view of their country home. She thought about the first time she had ever laid eyes on the place. It was a huge old white farmhouse with a spacious front porch. Eight rooms, the realtor had told them. Certainly more rooms than they needed, but Meghan had fallen in love with the big old house the moment she saw it.

It didn't need a lot of work either. It had been painted in recent years, and Meghan had envisioned how lovely it would look with hanging flower baskets gracing the front porch. It was set back quite a ways from the road too, a definite plus when you had a small child.

The front room was cozy with its tiny flower-print wallpaper and wide gleaming honey-pine floor boards. The charming country kitchen looked out over the backyard where a huge oak tree offered plenty of summer shade and the perfect place to hang a tire swing. The gently sloping property ran all the way down to a stand of tall pines and then an open field. When she had gazed out the kitchen window for the first time, Meghan had been lost in the moment, wondering if it was all real, or if it was a dream, until Rod coaxed her away from the peaceful view to follow the realtor through the rest of the house.

She was already sold on it though, even before she climbed the staircase to fall in love with the huge stone fireplace in the master bedroom. She was already imagining their life in this house, seeing herself reading stories to Rosie in the smaller bedroom, and hanging fresh laundry out on the old fashioned clothesline that had been left standing in the backyard.

When the realtor stepped out of the house to give them a few moments of privacy to talk things over, Rod knew by the excitement shining in Meghan's eyes that he didn't have to ask, but he did anyway. "What do you think, Honey?"

"It's perfect. It's just perfect. I love it!" she'd said, her face beaming. And from that moment, the house was as good as theirs. After they had made arrangements with the realtor to sign the paperwork, Meghan couldn't wait to pick up Rosie from the babysitter's and start making plans for their new home.

Rod watched Meghan slowly moving around the kitchen putting the groceries away. He could see the look of defeat in her expression and a shadow of anger swept over his face. He moved forward quickly, gripping her shoulders roughly, the hard look in his eyes revealing his stubborn streak. "Look Meghan, we're not giving up. Do you hear me?" he said through gritted teeth. "We're never going to give up!" When he saw the strength of his grip reflected in Meghan's face, he softened, pulling her close to him, crushing her against his broad chest, murmuring soothing words, his lips pressed against her hair.

When she finally pulled out of his embrace, she turned away rather than meet his gaze. He watched her busy herself with pulling the lunch meat and cheese from the fridge and begin putting together the cold cut sandwiches they would be having for lunch. Worry lines creased his forehead, and then an idea started to form in his mind as he watched Meghan take two plates from the cupboard.

While she was putting the sandwiches on the plates, Rod went up to their bedroom and returned a couple of minutes later with a stack of books in his arms. He set them down on the antique telephone table in the kitchen.

He cleared his throat. "Can you do me a favor?"

Meghan nodded her head without saying a word, opening the refrigerator to find something for them to drink with their meal.

"I should have brought these books with us this morning and returned them to the church's library, but I forgot. There's no hurry," he stressed, "but at some point they need to be returned." His hope was that sometime, when she was alone, she would see the books and be curious enough to open them and maybe find some positive ways of coping with her emotional pain.

Each morning after, when Meghan made her way down to the kitchen to make a pot of coffee and toast a couple slices of bread, she saw the books Rod had stacked on the telephone table. They were there each afternoon too, sitting on the little table just a few feet away as she made Rod's sandwiches and packed them with a cold drink for his lunch. And they were there in the early evening while Rod was working, every time she came into the kitchen to have a little something to eat. But she never opened them—never even picked one of them up.

She didn't need to open the books to know what they were about; she'd seen the titles on the ones he held in hand when he got into bed at night.

Now, standing in front of the historic white church with the books in her arms, Meghan took a breath and pulled one of the wide double doors open and entered. She made her way down the empty hallway feeling as though she didn't belong here. But she didn't feel much like she belonged anywhere. She felt like she was just a ghost of herself—an apparition. It was as if everything inside her had vanished on August 15th and now she was left with nothing but the faintest image of who she used to be.

Her high heels clicked on the shiny linoleum as she made her way down the long corridor to the church library, hugging the books close to her chest. One by one she put the books back on the shelves, filling the empty spaces. *These books can't help me*, she thought. *Nothing can help me*.

As she turned to leave the room, she stopped short, coming face to face with a huge picture of Jesus hanging on the wall right in front of her. His arms were outstretched as though he was reaching out for her. She stood there, frozen for a few seconds before looking away and leaving the room, the sound of her high heels once again clicking on the polished linoleum as she passed the pastor's office, a row of Sunday school rooms, and the sanctuary.

When she was nearing the front doors, she caught a glimpse of two women talking quietly, standing off to one side. As she got closer they stopped talking, but she could feel their eyes on her as she finally disappeared through the wide double doors.

Meghan couldn't fall sleep that night. She glanced at the bedside clock and saw it was just after midnight. She had taken the last sleeping pill the night before and had forgotten to have the prescription refilled. Rod lay sleeping beside her. Feeling restless, she climbed out of bed and went downstairs. She stepped out the kitchen door and stood on the back porch, breathing in the night air.

After a few minutes, she stepped off the porch and wandered down the path behind the house through the tall standing pines to the open field. It was a starry, starry night. The sky above her was a deep indigo blue with millions of twinkling lights. She remembered a night from a long time ago—a night just like this one—when she had scanned the dark sky searching it as if it held secrets. But tonight, the distant heaven revealed none of it's mysteries.

Still, something deep inside her refused to give up and just turn away and go back home. "Stubborn Irish," is what Rod would have called it. Instead, she spread her shawl beneath her and settled down on it until the darkness gave way to the muted colors of a salmon, rose, and coral tinted sky, and she began to feel a semblance of peace settling into her bones. It was either that or sheer exhaustion, she wasn't sure which. She finally stood and started towards home. When she reached the house, she climbed up the back porch steps and turned the doorknob.

Rod pulled the door open from the inside. "Meghan, where were you?" he asked, his face full of anxiety.

Meghan lifted her eyes to meet his and then lowered them to stare intently at the floor. "I went out for a walk…. That's all," she answered a little defensively.

Rod was incredulous. "In the middle of the night?! Are you crazy? There are wild animals out there at night. You could have been attacked. You could have been…" He took a deep breath to settle himself, and exhaled, trying to let go of some of the fear and frustration he was feeling. "When I woke up to use the bathroom, you weren't in bed, and you weren't anywhere in the house. I've been driving around for hours trying to find you. You had me worried sick. I was just about to call the police when I heard you on the back porch."

"I'm sorry Rod," Meghan said, noticing the car

keys still in his hand. "I didn't mean to upset you."

With her apology, Rod felt his anger diffuse and he reached out to put his arms around her. "That's okay Honey," he said soothingly. "I'm just glad you're okay. But please Meghan, don't ever do anything like that again, okay?"

Meghan sighed. "I won't Rod. I promise. I won't go out like that again without first letting you know where I'm going," she said.

Chapter 8

October gave way to a bleak, blustery November. Laurie pulled up a chair to keep her daily vigil at Richie's bedside, just as she had done the week before, and the weeks before that. She was always hoping there would be some sign of improvement, big or small, that she would be able to share with the boys. Ethan and Eric were constantly asking about their dad and it broke her heart to not have good news to bring back to them. As this afternoon wore on, it looked like today wasn't going to be different than any of the other days before it.

"Richie, Honey," she said softly, placing her hand over his. "It's me—Laurie. I'm right here, and I want you to know that I love you… I love you so much Richie. And the boys love you. They ask about you every day and they ask God to help you get well in their prayers every night. Please squeeze my hand if you can hear me, Richie. Please open your eyes…. Please wake up."

But again, today, there was no response from him, and when she couldn't bear watching him lie there so still any longer, she leaned over and kissed him on his cheek. "I'll be back again tomorrow, Richie. I love you so much, sweetheart. We're not going to give up on you," she whispered, her face still just inches from his.

The dark and dreary days of November gradually slid—along with the falling temperature—into a typical New England December. It was the week before Christmas and a light snow was falling, snowflakes like tiny intricate patterns of lace melting as they touched the ground. Laurie watched them through the big bay window while waiting for Pammy to arrive to watch Elizabeth so she could go to the hospital to visit Richie.

She had been grateful that her mom and dad had taken over the responsibility of picking out a fresh cut Christmas tree, hauling it home on the roof of their car, and then setting it up in the corner of the living room. They had enlisted Ethan and Eric to help them string multiple strands of multi-colored lights and decorate it with the family's collection of Christmas tree ornaments. But even with the Christmas tree set up, and the sound of the

Christmas carols floating out from the radio, it still didn't feel like Christmas. It just wouldn't be Christmas without having Richie home to celebrate it with her and the children.

When Pammy's car pulled into the drive, Laurie turned away from the window. "She's here Mom, so we can go now." Laurie watched her mother come into the room carrying Elizabeth in her arms.

"She just fell asleep," Dee said while laying her down in her crib.

Laurie was glad it was the weekend because that meant she didn't have to go to the hospital alone. At least there would be someone to keep her company while she sat in Richie's hospital room.

Pammy knocked lightly on the front door before opening it, bringing in the scent of the wintery weather as she came through the door. Laurie fumbled in her purse for her car keys, anxious to be on her way.

"Elizabeth's asleep in her crib," Laurie said while she and her mom were putting on their coats and scarves. "There's a bottle of formula in the fridge in case she wakes up while we're away. There's some left over takeout pizza in there too, for you and the boys if you get hungry. We won't be gone long," she added, pulling on her gloves.

"Don't worry about us," Pammy said reassuringly as Laurie and Dee were walking out the door. "We'll be just fine."

Once inside the hospital, they crossed the lobby and walked down the hallway and took the elevator up to the fourth floor. When they stepped into Richie's room, his bed was empty, and all the monitors with all their quiet hums and beeps were shut off.

Laurie turned to her mother, all the color draining from her face. "What's going on?!" she asked, her voice rising in panic. "Where's Richie?!"

Dee searched for something to say, but just then an ICU nurse passing by the room saw them and stopped. She quickly entered the room and put a reassuring hand on Laurie's shoulder. "It's okay Laurie, they just moved Richie to another room about twenty minutes ago," she said. "They called your house phone, but there was no answer. Then they tried your cell, but..."

Laurie instinctively reached into the side pocket of her purse, but her cell phone wasn't there. "I must have left my cell phone at home," she said, feeling guilty. "Is he okay?"

The nurse smiled. "Don't worry Laurie, he's okay. One of the nurses was checking his vital signs just a little while ago and he opened his eyes. Just like that!" she said, snapping her fingers. "I guess you could call it a Christmas miracle. The first thing he said was that he was hungry."

"That sounds like Richie!" Laurie said trying to laugh, but then she began to cry.

Tears filled Dee's eyes too, and the nurse searched inside her pockets for a few tissues, giving them a moment to regain their composure before she spoke again. "They moved him to the second floor, room 202. And I'm sure he'd love to see you."

Dee was slightly out of breath from trying to keep up with Laurie as she made her way down the hall to Ritchie's room. When they entered the room, he was sitting half-way up in bed, propped up with a few pillows supporting his neck and shoulders.

"Richie!" Laurie exclaimed. "I can hardly believe it," she said rushing across the room and sitting down on the edge of the bed. "You're really awake!"

He smiled at her and took her hands in his. "Yes."

They just looked at each other, and then Laurie broke the silence. "What did the doctor say about your condition when he saw you after you woke up?" she asked.

"The doctor said I'm very lucky. I don't seem to have lost any part of my memory, but they're going to run some tests just to make sure. Then they're going to get me up and out of bed to see if I can walk on my own, and check to see whether I have any problems with mobility. Things like that. One thing's for sure, I shouldn't have any trouble eating. I'm starving! What time is dinner served around here, anyway?"

Laurie laughed and Dee joined in with laughter of her own.

"Well, we're sure glad to see that you're back to being yourself again, Richie. You sure had us all worried there for a while. This is such a big relief," Dee sighed. "Now... I'm sure the two of you would like a few moments to be alone, so I'm going to leave and make a few phone calls. I'm going to call Daddy first, and then I'll call Pammy to share the good news," she said.

"Please ask Daddy and Pammy not to say anything to the boys about Richie," Laurie said before Dee turned to leave the room. "I want to be the one to tell them the news."

"Of course Dear. I'll let them both know that

you'd like to be the one to share the good news with the twins," Dee said.

After Dee had stepped out of the room, Richie's eyes searched Laurie's for a moment. "I'm so sorry about the accident Laur. You weren't hurt, were you? During the accident, I mean..."

"No Richie, I wasn't hurt," she said, giving him a small smile.

"No one would tell me anything about what happened... And the baby?" he asked tentatively.

"The baby wasn't hurt either Honey," she said reassuringly. "We have a beautiful baby girl. I named her Elizabeth, just like we had talked about before everything happened. I'll bring her in later so you can see her. And the twins, of course! Ethan and Eric have missed you so much. They're going to be so excited when I tell them that their prayers have finally been answered!"

"Great!" Richie said smiling broadly. "I can't wait to see my boys, and my baby girl!"

There was a quiet knock on the door and Dee peeked in. "Can I come back in?"

"Of course!" Laurie beamed.

An hour later, after giving Richie a hug good-bye, Dee stepped out of the room again, this time to give

Laurie a little privacy to say good-bye to her husband.

When Laurie finally stepped out into the hall, she went back into the room to give Richie another hug and kiss goodbye. As she was leaving the room for the second time, she looked back at him. "I'll ask one of the nurses to bring you something to eat to hold you until it's time for your dinner."

Richie smiled. "Thanks Laur. That would be great. And by the way, did I tell you that I love you?"

Laurie breezed through the front door ahead of Dee with snowflakes still clinging to her coat. "Thank you for watching Elizabeth, Pammy. Are the boys home yet?" She asked.

Pammy shook her head. "No. They're sledding on the big hill behind the old high school with some of their friends."

"Good! I can't wait to see the expressions on their faces when I tell them!" Laurie said, as she scooped Elizabeth up into her arms and buried her face in the soft folds of her infant daughter's neck, breathing in her freshly bathed baby scent. Then she straightened and gazed down at Elizabeth, excitement shining in her eyes. "Daddy's coming home, sweetheart. Your daddy's coming home!"

"How's Richie doing?" Pammy asked.

"He said he feels fine," Laurie beamed. "The doctors are running tests, of course, but Richie said that when they're finished with all that, he's going to take a long hot shower and shave himself, and then have his dinner. The doctor said the tests are only going to take a few hours, so I'm going to go out and do some more Christmas shopping! Mom said she'll take over now and watch Elizabeth while I'm gone."

"But I thought you said you were done with all of your shopping," Pammy said.

"I was, but I haven't bought anything for Richie yet. The boys should be home by then, and then I'll bundle Elizabeth up and take her and the boys to see their dad. He said he can't wait to see her—and his sons of course. I can't wait to see him again either. One of the doctors said that if everything checks out, Richie may be ready to come home as early as tomorrow!"

Chapter 9

On the loading dock, the December wind was punishing. It stung Rod's face, and his lungs ached with every breath he took while he ran in and out of the production sites, loading the truck as fast as he could. When he'd finished loading, he drove up to the magazine in the woods.

He left the truck's engine running so the heater and defroster would keep the windshield from icing over, and stepped back out into the freezing night. Now he had to shovel his way in before stacking the hand truck with the boxes of dynamite and rolling them in. When he had finished, he rolled the hand truck back out to the truck and put it on the lift gate.

By this time his breathing was labored, but he knew that the harder he worked, the sooner he'd be done. Then he could get out of the cold and back to the warm office where he would enter his report of the night's activity into the computer. It had been a long hard night working alone in the cold and dark, and by the time he reached the office door, he couldn't wait to wrap things up and punch the time clock.

When he made it home, he headed straight to the bathroom to take a long shower. The steamy, hot water felt great. After he'd showered, he climbed into bed and was finally able to relax. But there was something missing. He needed to feel the closeness, the intimacy with his wife that they'd lost. He needed to take her into his arms. He needed to feel her soft skin against his. He needed to breathe in the light scent of her perfume and forget about everything else in the world, except the two of them wrapped in each other's arms. He needed to lose himself in her love.

Beside him, Meghan lay on her side facing away from him. He listened to her soft breathing and reached for her, gently resting his hand on her shoulder. He waited, hoping she would turn over, snuggle up against him, and lay her head on his chest the way she used to.

But just like all the other nights since Rosie had disappeared, Meghan lay there, perfectly still, pretending to be asleep.

The next day, Rod was standing outside his

supervisor's office wondering why he'd been summoned to a private meeting before starting his shift. He tried to think of anything he could have done wrong during the previous night's work, but couldn't come up with anything. He knocked lightly on the door.

"Come in," Warren said, motioning Rod to have a seat in the chair in front of his desk when he entered the room. "The reason I called you in is because we have a very serious situation on our hands. A box of dynamite from one of the shipments you loaded the other night has gone missing... and I'm wondering if you have any idea what could have happened to it."

Warren paused for a long moment before he went on. "Of course you know our foremost concern is that the powder could have somehow been stolen by terrorists, but since the shortage was discovered by the person on the receiving end of a shipment you loaded, we want to hear what you have to say about the discrepancy," he said, looking Rod squarely in the eyes.

Rod felt the weight of Warren's unspoken accusation as heavily as if he had been punched in the chest. After all these years, how could Warren possibly think...? He struggled to think of something to say that would clear him of any suspicion of wrong doing or mishandling of the missing explosive, but he was at a complete loss. He tried to remember exactly what he'd done that night.

Unsatisfied by Rod's lack of response, Warren continued. "There have already been some closed door meetings with the higher-ups. And of course, the ATF has been called in to investigate. They'll be working with management, pulling files, doing an inventory, and verifying shipments to see if they can turn up anything. They're going to be questioning people at every level here too. I'm sure they'll be speaking with you very soon. I just wanted to give you a heads up," he said soberly.

"Thanks Warren, I appreciate it," Rod said on his way out of the room. Maybe Warren was in his corner after all, but at the moment he couldn't really be sure. After closing the door behind him, he made quick strides down the hall and then out of the building. His meeting with Warren had already put him behind schedule.

It was snowing like crazy and getting colder by the minute, and Rod just knew it was going to be another night from hell. He loaded the truck and started making his rounds, going from shipping and receiving, and then to other departments and buildings, dropping off the supplies they'd ordered. By the time he was done jumping in and out of the truck, he was numb from the cold.

Trying to stay focused on the tasks at hand while the huge problem of the missing dynamite kept pressing toward the forefront of his mind had been exhausting. But finally, it was time for him to go into the office and enter his work into the computer and close up for the night.

As he pulled out of the employee parking lot, he knew this was going to one of those nights when he wouldn't be able to leave his troubles at work behind him. Tonight, it would be following him all the way home.

All along the roads, power lines swayed. When he finally made it home, he stepped out of his truck into the empty cold darkness. The cold wind blew around the eaves of the old farmhouse and howled through the barren branches of the birch trees. Above the front porch, huge icicles hung like crystal daggers from the roof.

After he climbed into bed and laid there for what seemed like an eternity, he turned onto his side and saw the digits on the alarm clock glowing 3 a.m.

Beside him, Meghan lay wrapped up in a thick white comforter to escape the chill of the wintry night.

He'd been trying to sleep for the past two hours, but his mind kept going over and over everything that had happened the night the dynamite went missing until his head hurt. Had he made a mistake? In his hurry to get the job done on that bitter cold night, had he misplaced the box of missing explosive powder? Had he been the one responsible for his division—and himself—coming under the scrutiny of the ATF?

Sooner than he expected, Rod found himself sitting inside Warren's office again. When he saw the hard look in Warren's eyes, he felt a wave of apprehension crash through his chest. Two men wearing ATF uniforms stood beside Warren's desk.

"Look Rod, I'll get straight to the point. We've recovered the missing powder." The look in Warren's eyes was accusatory. "Do you have any idea where we might have found it?" he asked.

"No sir," Rod answered, trying to keep the fear out of his voice.

"Well, it just so happens that when we searched your locker, lo and behold, there it was. What do you have to say for yourself?"

Rod looked from Warren to the two men. One of them had his hand resting on the butt of his gun. Knots of tension formed at Rod's temples. "That's not true," he shouted, suddenly angry. "You're lying! Or... or maybe someone's trying to set me up!" He didn't know what to say, his anger now clouded with confusion. "It doesn't make any sense."

"Oh, really?" Warren asked. "Please explain to me how anyone else would have had access to your locker."

"I don't know. I... I... honestly don't know," Rod said, feeling defeated. "I guess I'm going to have to call my lawyer." He stood to leave the office to make a phone call, but the two ATF officers quickly positioned themselves between him and the door.

One of the men pulled out a set of handcuffs from behind his back. Rod tried to back away, but fell backwards over the chair behind him, tumbling to the floor. He awoke with a jerk, covered in a cold sweat, and lay there for a minute waiting for his heart to stop pounding. Then he climbed out of bed and made his way into the bathroom.

Leaning over the sink, he splashed cold water onto his face. When he looked into the mirror, he saw dark half-moon circles beneath his eyes and wondered how much more pressure could he take. He could feel himself getting closer and closer to a breaking point. Why was all of this happening to him? Had he somehow brought it on himself?

He was used to being an excellent problem solver, but ever since that horrific night in August, his life had taken a sudden and drastic turn for the worse. And the circumstances that he now found himself in were beyond his capabilities of solving. If he could ever clear his thoughts enough to escape some of the turmoil that was threatening to overwhelm him, he was going to do some serious soul searching. At least he only had one day of work left before the weekend. Hopefully, those two days off would give him a chance to recharge his batteries—at least a little.

On Saturday, the weather had warmed up above the freezing mark, but the strong winds of the night before had torn branches off the birches and the old oak in the backyard. Rod went outside and surveyed the damage. He decided an ax would do the job, and chopped the fallen branches into smaller pieces, hauling them across the yard to the wood shed.

When he went back into the house, he took his forty caliber pistol, some ammunition, and a couple extra clips outside and set some targets up in the back yard. He methodically loaded, aimed, and fired the pistol, reloading and firing over and over again, hitting the center of the targets repeatedly. When he ran out of ammo, he went back into the house and broke down the pistol to clean and oil it while it was still warm. By late evening, he fell into bed exhausted, but at least he was finally able to get a decent night's sleep.

On Sunday morning, Rod worked hard on convincing Meghan to go to church with him. Sometimes she would feel up to going and sometimes she wouldn't. He usually succeeded on days when it wasn't bitterly cold outside. The cold weather seemed to bother her a lot more since....

Sitting in one of the smooth wooden pews, Rod felt himself relax as he shifted his focus away from his worries and felt a much needed peace find its way into his soul. But while everybody was singing a hymn, Meghan got up from her seat and disappeared into the ladies room. She was gone for much longer than Rod had thought she would be, and he was beginning to wonder if she was okay. When she finally returned to her place beside him, he could see that she had been crying. Sometimes being in church made her weep and Rod tried as best as he could to comfort her.

After church, Rod decided to try to take her mind off of things, so on their way home he pulled into the parking lot of a restaurant that had just opened up in the center of town. After the waitress had taken their order, Rod noticed that Meghan's gaze was trained on a young girl with long dark hair who must have been around eight or nine years old. She was standing with her back to them, several tables away from where they were seated.

"Rosie..." Meghan whispered, a look of hopeful determination filling her eyes.

She was out of her seat before Rod could stop her and making her way quickly across the room. He reached her just after she had placed a hand on the young girl's shoulder. The young girl turned around and looked up at Meghan. Embarrassed, Rod apologized to the girl's parents, who had each placed a protective hand of their own on their daughter's shoulder. Then he gently took Meghan by the arm and led her back to their table.

"I just had to see for myself," Meghan said in a feeble voice. "I just had to make sure."

The next afternoon, Rod dressed for work and

slipped his cell phone into his shirt pocket. There had been a voice mail from Warren, telling Rod to meet him in his office as soon as he had punched in. Instinctively, Rod knew this was about the missing dynamite, and immediately felt the tension knotting up between his shoulder blades. There wasn't any time to call Warren now. All he had was the half hour ride it would take to get to work on time.

Rod wondered if Warren had planned it that way. Maybe whatever he had to say was important enough—or serious enough—that he didn't want to discuss it over the phone. Anxiously, Rod grabbed his car keys and headed for the door. A half hour later, he knocked lightly on Warren's office door, having gone over everything that could have possibly happened on the bitter cold night the dynamite had gone missing and still coming up with nothing.

When he entered the office, Warren waived a hand at the chair in front of his desk, motioning him to sit down. After Rod was seated, Warren cleared his throat and began. "The ATF has completed their investigation. I have a copy of their report sitting right here on top of my desk. According to this report, the missing powder has been recovered, and it explains in detail what caused the inventory shortage.

"As you probably remember, the morning after you had loaded the boxes into the warehouse, it began snowing and had continued to snow for the remainder of the day. It wasn't an easy trip for the driver to make under those conditions. By the time the driver was in Canada, the snow was really coming down. The further north he drove, the heavier it snowed until there were a few feet of fresh snow on the ground and visibility was… well, it was a complete white out. That's when the truck driver called and said the truck had slid off the road. We had to send out another truck and driver to help him transfer the boxes of dynamite onto the second truck.

"It turned out that while they were unloading the truck, one of the boxes slid off the back of the truck and fell into the deep snow. They didn't see it happen, and because of the blizzard-like weather conditions, it was covered with snow before they had a chance to see it. As soon as the drivers were informed about the missing powder they realized what must have happened and drove all the way back to Canada to locate the exact spot where the truck had been dug out of the snow. It was no easy task with the snow covering everything and there was no guarantee that the box was going to be there, but eventually they found it. The ATF was on the scene and recovered the product, so everything is squared away now."

Chapter 10

On Christmas morning Richie was holding baby Elizabeth in his arms as he and Laurie sat cross-legged on the floor beside the Christmas tree waiting for Ethan and Eric to wake up so that they could all open their gaily wrapped presents together. Laurie gazed solemnly at the baby nestled in the crook of Richie's arm.

"She has your brown hair and your blue eyes, Richie. She even has your smile. She reminded me so much of you that it hurt every time I looked at her."

"She *is* a beautiful baby," Richie said with a glint of humor in his eyes.

Laurie's brows drew together, a frown on face. "You may find it amusing now, but it certainly wasn't amusing when you were hooked up to all of those machines…. I really thought I was going to lose you."

"I'm sorry you had to go through all that, and I know it was really hard, especially with having the baby to take care of. But I'm okay now and everything is going to be great from now on," Richie promised.

Laurie looked at him, searching his eyes. "*Are* you okay, Richie? Are you really okay?" she asked as if she was afraid to believe that everything was fine now.

"Remember what the doctor told us about the test results, Laur. Everything checked out fine. I'm practically as good as new," he said smiling, but noticing the serious expression still clouding her face. "Come here," he said, holding his free arm out to her. "We're all together now and everything is going to be fine, you'll see. I've got my two girls—and my two boys," he said as he wrapped his arm around Laurie's shoulders. "I'm a very happy man—and a very lucky one too."

Laurie's frown faded and was replaced with a smile. "This is the best Christmas ever, Richie," she said, sounding completely contented.

Richie unfolded his arm from around her and tilted her chin up so he could look into her eyes. "If you think that this is something, just wait until you meet me underneath the mistletoe later," he said with a smug half-smile. He winked at her and she couldn't keep herself from laughing. Just then, two sleepy-eyed twelve-year-old boys stumbled out of their bedroom and into the living room.

"Hold that thought," Richie said with a conspiratorial look in his eyes. Then he turned toward his blond-haired, blue-eyed identical twin sons and said with a twinkle in his eye, "Merry Christmas boys!"

Chapter 11

A dazzling Christmas tree strung with frost-covered twinkling lights and a myriad of delicately hand painted ornaments sat on the snow covered lawn in front of the city hall. It was surrounded by heavily coated and glove-clad, ruddy-cheeked villagers waiting for the winter festival to begin.

Rosie stood among them with Sergi and Valdoma, watching as a group of men rode their lively horses, evergreens and festive ribbons braided into their manes and tails. Bright red tassels hung from their bridles while handmade cloth saddles displayed colorful patterns of holly berries and snow birds.

Next, a group of younger men with white cloth horse heads attached to their waists "galloped" onto the stage that had been set up for a spirited "dance of the horses". Their feet moved quickly in unison, their boots kicking high into the air, hands slapping heels in time with the music. When they had "galloped" off the stage, a group of men, this time hidden inside bear costumes, were led by their gypsy "trainer" through the crowd to the spine tingling excitement of the young and old alike.

When the day's festivities were over, Sergi, Valdoma, and Rosie made their way home for a meal of roasted pork, potatoes, and black pudding.

Two days before Christmas, Rosie and her companions hurried gaily along the village streets for a night of caroling. Christmas lights were strung along roof lines and beautifully decorated trees twinkled behind front windows as they went from door to door with shining eyes and rosy cheeks.

Rosie was being swept along in the center of the young carolers carrying a pole with a huge paper star on top that had a picture of the nativity scene in its center. When a door opened, the children sang their Christmas carols with upturned faces to adults listening from just inside their homes. When they had finished spreading their joyous tidings of Christmas cheer, they were each rewarded with a piece of fruit, a handful of nuts, or a cookie. As the winter night turned colder, Rosie and her friend Rahela broke away from the group and headed off towards their own homes.

As they drew nearer to Sergi's and Valdoma's

house, Rahela stopped for a moment and listened. Then she turned to Rosie. "I can hear your ta-ta calling for you," she said.

"My ta-ta?" Rosie asked, sounding confused.

"Yes, your ta-ta. You know... your father," Rahela explained.

Rosie lifted her eyes to ponder the nativity scene inside the star while a shadow passed over her face. Then she slowly lowered her eyes to the ground. "He's not my ta-ta," she mumbled.

Rahela cocked her head to one side. "What do you mean he's not your ta-ta?" she asked.

"Oh... never mind," Rosie said, lifting her eyes to meet Rahela's. Then she turned and ran in the direction of Sergi's voice.

On Christmas Eve, sitting in front of the twinkling Christmas tree, Rosie opened the presents she had received from Sergi, Valdoma, and Baba. From the first gift box, she lifted a beautiful white linen shirt that Valdoma had embellished with red and green embroidery. Beneath it, nestled amongst the festively colored tissue paper, lay a long red woolen skirt. A new woolen coat was among the other gifts that she had opened, along with the hand-sewn cloth doll that Baba had outfitted with the identical embroidered Christmas shirt and long red skirt that Rosie had just received. From Sergi, there was a carved wooden horse that remarkably resembled Magic.

Early Christmas morning, Valdoma and Rosie headed for the barn, each carrying a small bucket of warm, sweet mash for the horses. They stopped for a moment to watch the birds hungrily peck at the special holiday treat of pinecones smeared full of lard and bird seed that were hanging from the low branches of the trees. They waved to Ceasar and Emelian who were on their way to the lions' enclosure.

"Ceasar! Emelian!" Valdoma called to them. "The coffee is already on. When you have finished with the lions, come up to the house and have breakfast with us. There is plenty for us to eat."

Inside the barn, Valdoma and Rosie watched the horses enjoy their sweet mash until every last bit of grain was gone. They took the wreaths they had decorated with berries down from hooks on the barn walls, and placed them over the horses' heads onto their necks before turning the horses out to the outdoor ring.

When they returned to the house, they were met

with the aromas of strong coffee, and the mititei, eggs, and potatoes Sergi was frying in a heavy skillet. This morning, they would also have the doughnuts and cozanac bread that Valdoma and Rosie had made the day before along with their breakfast.

Throughout the day, Christmas carolers came and went. Sergi, Valdoma, and Baba listened to their beautiful voices from just inside the doorway, handing out holiday treats to each caroler before they went on their way while Rosie sat nearby, playing with her new toys.

Valdoma and Baba were sitting at the table enjoying another thick slice of cozanac bread along with their tea. Still dressed in her traditional Romanian Christmas costume, Rosie sat down on the woven rug beside the Christmas tree to play with her toys. As the day slowly faded to night, a light snow began to fall. From inside the window, Rosie watched quietly as a fresh layer of snow covered the ground, her eyelids beginning to grow heavy. She stood and sleepily made her way down the hall to her bedroom.

Chapter 12

Meghan tried not to think about the small pile of Christmas cards lying on the kitchen table. They had accumulated throughout the week, coming in each day with the afternoon mail, reminding her just how empty the house was right now. There were no holiday decorations adorning the old farm house, and no presents under a lighted Christmas tree as there had been in years past. She tried not to think about how different this Christmas would've been if only... but the tears began to fall from her eyes anyway. She wiped them away with the back of her hand when she heard Rod coming in through the kitchen door.

He shook the snowflakes from his hair, went to the coffee maker to pour himself a cup of coffee, and sighed as he sat down at the kitchen table. Although they had received many offers from caring family and friends to come and spend the afternoon with them, they had declined them all, choosing instead to spend the day at home. Now, the long hours of the day slowly ticked by. When the sun was finally setting, Meghan breathed a sigh of relief at having made it through the day.

Rod had convinced her to attend the candlelight service with him, and now handed her her coat with an encouraging smile.

Inside the semi-darkness of the Baptist church, anointed music flowed out from the organ. The voices of men and women dressed in crimson and white choir robes were like the voices of angels filling the sanctuary, gloriously proclaiming the miraculous birth of Christ.

On their way home, the snow sparkled under the moonlight, while colored lights that had been strung along the entire outline of many of the houses made them look like magical gumdrop houses. Meghan gazed at them without really seeing them. The only thing that had made a lasting impression on her senses this Christmas night was the bone chilling cold she felt getting in and out of the car. When they walked from Rod's car to the house, it felt like it was at least ten degrees colder than it had been when they had left.

Once they were in the house, Rod went upstairs

and changed out of his church clothes, and then went out to the back porch to grab logs from the wood pile while Meghan stood at the stove pouring boiling water over a tea bag. He came back in carrying an armful of logs and headed up the stairs to the fireplace in the bedroom. Meghan followed him up and sat in the center of the bed sipping her tea while the cup gently warmed her hands, watching Rod patiently coax the fire to life.

When the fire was going on its own, he left the room to get more firewood. As she stared at the fire, she thought about all the Christmas cards again—the only evidence of Christmas that had been in the house this holiday season.

The card lying on top of the pile had been from Stan, her former boss. He was older now, somewhere in his mid-seventies. She imagined him spending this holiday season settled into a rocking chair with one of his many grandchildren sitting on his knee, the deep snow outside his window making a soft blanket around his house.

She thought of others too. Ted, wearing a jolly red and white Santa's cap as he served up his droll sense of humor to his regular customers at the diner. There was Robbie too. Sweet young Robbie with that endless sense of searching shining through his innocent blue eyes. And Laurie.... Meghan's heart grew heavy remembering all her old friends from what seemed like such a long time ago.

She heard the back door close and shifted herself over to her side of the bed. She heard Rod's footfalls on the stairs and set her teacup down on the small maple nightstand beside the bed and lay down, turning onto her side to try and get some sleep. Now she thought of the portrait of Myles. With her eyes closed, she imagined him with his ruggedly handsome features and placid grey eyes, coming home with his hunting hat in his hand, to the little grey bungalow and his faithful and ever-hopeful wife Stevie.

Chapter 13

The gypsy performers traveling season began with a tour in their own country. Rosie sat offstage with Baba, hidden in the shadows while the clowns amused the crowd with their silly antics. The night at the circus was filled with all the spell binding acts anyone could possibly imagine. Rosie watched, along with the audience, as the man with slick black hair swallowed the flaming sword, and the trapeze artists swung from the high wires, death-defyingly somersaulting through the air. Then the bears and the lions took their turn captivating the audience, followed by the gypsies on their horses.

When the circus performance was over, the night vibrated with the sounds of lively folk music and laughter in the camp. The women danced by the fire. Some of the children danced too, twirling long scarves and spinning around and around in circles. Rahela, with her thick black hair and impish grin, ran to Rosie. She pulled Rosie by the arm and led her to where the other children were dancing, coaxing her until she gave in and joined them in their dance.

The fire burned steadily, clouds of blue-black smoke rising up into the air. Babies cried softly as they were being carried to the wagons. Rosie, sitting on an old tree stump, looked up into the sky and saw a shooting star. "Look, Baba!" she exclaimed, pointing up into the clear dark night.

In a hushed voice, Baba corrected her. "You must never do that again Raisa, for when a star shoots across the sky, it means that a thief has run away. If you point to the star, he is likely to be caught."

"Oh," Rosie said in a small voice. She gazed quietly at the sky for a long time, pondering Baba's words until her eyelids grew heavy and she drifted off to sleep, listening to the Romani's animated banter and songs.

Chapter 14

Little patches of snow still covered the ground in the shady spots under the birch trees, but somehow the sparrows must have known it was the first day of spring, for they sang their little hearts out from their perches on the thin bare branches. There was still a lingering chill in the air, which made it a good day to get home projects done inside rather than outside. When the phone rang, Rod was in the middle of working on fixing a broken pipe underneath the kitchen sink. He dropped everything to quickly grab the receiver. It was only Meghan's mom making her weekly call to ask how they were getting on, but every time the phone rang he still hoped.

"Hi Mom... Yes, we're okay. How are things with you and Dad?" He nodded his head as if agreeing with what Colleen had just said, and then lowered his voice to an apologetic tone. "I'd put Meghan on, but... she's exhausted and upstairs resting right now. Her friend Laurie stopped by this morning and they had a good cry together. I hope it helped Meghan a little with the healing process, but I don't know if that's even possible at this point.

He listened. "Maybe," he said shaking his head, "but I've read a lot of books on it, and I've gone to counseling. They all say the same thing—it takes time to heal. But if you ask me, there isn't enough time left in the world for that to happen...."

After a break in his side of the conversation, he went on. "Yes, it was good to see Laurie again. She said she hadn't come out sooner because she wasn't sure how Meghan would feel about being around her when she was so pregnant. Then there was the accident and Richie being in a coma for so long."

He paused again, listening to Colleen's end of the conversation before going on. "Laurie said he's doing fine now. There doesn't seem to be any permanent damage." Then after a moment he said "No, thank God the boys weren't in the car at the time. They were in school when it happened."

After they'd both run out of things to say and had promised to talk again soon, Rod hung up the phone, remembering how relieved he'd been when Meghan had told him that Richie had come out of the coma and was okay.

He and Richie had become good friends over the years. And Rod didn't make friends easily. He knew that people thought of him as a hard man. He knew it was because he did most things with an intensity that few of his peers possessed. He was precise, and paid acute attention to detail, but that was why he was so well suited for the line of work he was in. When it came to working with dynamite, one wrong move or careless mistake could cost him his life.

Maybe Meghan was the only person who'd ever really seen the other side of him—the tender side. She'd seen that side of him when he'd picked the last summer rose from the generation's old rose bush that had grown in his yard and handed it to her under the moonlight. And when he gently took his infant daughter out of her arms at four o'clock in the morning after his night shift at the plant so she could get some sleep. She'd also seen it in the look of relief on his face when he'd found out that Richie was going to be okay.

At their wedding, Richie had been Rod's best man, and Laurie had been Meghan's maid of honor. It had been a simple wedding in the small country church on the outskirts of town. Glowing white candles resting inside rustic hickory-wood lanterns had lined both sides of the steps that led up to the front of the church. Hundreds of tiny white lights had shone through the intertwining grapevines of the heart-shaped wreath placed on the church's front door. Inside the church, huge white satin bows had graced the ends of the pews.

As Rod stood at the altar and waited while his bride-to-be made her way up the aisle to meet him, strong emotions had caught in his throat. She had been breathtaking in a pure white gossamer gown, wearing a crown of wildflowers in her hair. Her bright blue eyes had shone with the unmistakable light of love.

Meghan had smiled at Rod when she arrived at his side. He made a handsome groom in his black and white tuxedo. His dark hair had been neatly trimmed and anticipation had been clearly etched in his blue-green eyes. When the ceremony was over, and everyone was standing outside the church, Rod and Meghan had released two snow white doves and watched them fly off together up into the clear blue sky, their wings lifting them higher and higher towards heaven.

She had become pregnant during the first year of their marriage, a fact she was delighted with. Her ob/gyn hadn't been quite as delighted though. She was 40 years old, and there were risk factors associated with her age. But God had allowed Meghan to become pregnant, and she had all the faith in the world that everything was going to be fine. After all, she ate healthy food most of the time, and exercised every day. And for the most part, it had been an easy pregnancy. She did have awful morning sickness though. Actually, it had lasted much longer than the morning. It lasted all the way through dinner time—for almost a full three months. But it would be worth it in the end, and that's what she kept reminding herself.

During her last trimester, her legs were so swollen that she couldn't get comfortable in bed at night. By then she had begun to feel like she was going to pregnant forever, but finally, her water broke and Rod drove her to the hospital. Eight uncomfortable and exhausting hours later, she held her seven-and-a-half pound baby girl, snugly wrapped in a soft pink blanket, in her arms.

She was surprised by the baby's very dark—almost black hair. She had Rod's rich complexion, but the same tiny rosebud-shaped mouth Meghan had had as an infant, so she already bore a beautiful resemblance to both her mommy and her daddy.

And it was true what the Bible had said about how a mother forgets the pain of laboring to bring forth a new life, for the joy that her child has been born into the world. Meghan nursed her baby and prayed for her, believing that everything was going to be wonderful now that the pregnancy was finally over. Her baby was here, and she could finally cuddle and play with her, and watch her grow. And she did watch Rosie grow, first from a chubby toddler with dimpled cheeks and elbows to a happy, playful, and inquisitive preschooler, and then into a bright and energetic seven-year-old.

But everything changed, and where was Meghan's faith now? That was the unanswered question that hung in the air around her, a question she didn't want to think about. She knew that having faith wasn't always easy, that sometimes faith was a fight, but these days she just felt too weak and too tired to fight. Instead, she turned her thoughts over to the conversation she'd had with Stevie earlier that day.

Stevie had called her and invited her to go on a picnic, letting Meghan know she'd already planned everything out. She had fried up a batch of chicken drumsticks, filled a container with homemade potato salad, wrapped up a batch of freshly baked oatmeal raisin cookies, and filled a jug with iced tea with fresh mint.

"There's a special place I go to sometimes," Stevie had said, sounding as though she was excited to share her favorite spot with Meghan.

Meghan didn't feel like she was up to any type of adventure, but she couldn't find it in her heart to turn her friend's invitation down. So now she was in her bedroom changing into a pair of faded jeans, a loose comfortable T-shirt, and weathered tawny hiking boots. When she started up the driveway to Stevie's house, she could see Stevie sitting on her front porch steps, a white wicker picnic basket sitting beside her.

They walked quietly along the side of the road for nearly an hour when Stevie turned onto a path leading into the forest. Meghan sighed, knowing that if Stevie had told her how long it was going to take them to reach their destination, she'd probably have declined the invitation. Now they were hiking through the cool green, pine-scented woods. Finally, Stevie stopped and started spreading out a blanket on the fairly level forest floor.

Taking in the beauty of her new surroundings, Meghan was awestruck by the sight of the huge waterfall on the other side of the brook. She stood and watched crystal clear water tumble down over wide stone ledges—nature's own stairway—before spilling into a deep, dark pool. Settling down on the blanket, Meghan had to admit to herself that it had been worth the effort to reach this spot in the woods. The falls were beautiful, actually breath taking, and as she sat there watching the water fall, she could feel a calm starting to settle within her soul.

After sitting together quietly for a while, both of them apparently deep in their own thoughts, Stevie spoke softly. "When I was still a child, but old enough to go off by myself, I used to come here. I happened to find it one summer afternoon when I was out exploring. I rode my bike through the entrance to the forest and hid it behind a big hemlock tree. I followed the path here, and then hiked over to Emmons Pond. I used to sit beside the pond watching the big brown box turtles with their yellow and green speckled shells. There were plenty of frogs perched on the edge of the pond too, but as soon as I tried to catch one of them, they'd always leap straight into the pond. There were red salamanders too, skittering over half-rotted sections of fallen tree branches, or darting out from under clumps of decaying leaves.

"I used to spend whole days exploring the hidden nooks and crevices of Hurricane Brook, following the rushing water down the twisting chutes, slides, and waterfalls until I reached the covered bridge. I'd stop halfway across and look out one of the openings in the side wall of the bridge and watch the water rushing downstream.

"It was quite an adventure for an inquisitive young girl like me. There's even an actual cave in these woods, and an old abandoned building too. I used to pretend I lived in that building and that it was my home. I'd stand at the front door and know that all of the forest and all of the creatures living in it belonged to me." Stevie laughed out loud at her own childhood imaginings. "Well then, shall we enjoy our picnic lunch?" she asked as she opened the wicker basket.

A few hours later, the first shadows began to reach into the heart of the forest, so Meghan and Stevie packed up and started the long trek back home. And that night, for the first time in a very long time, when Meghan's head hit her pillow, she fell into a sound sleep—the long hike, the fresh air, the picnic fare, and the waterfall actually having done her some good.

The next day, Rod spent the afternoon chopping firewood until his shoulders and back ached. He needed the physical labor to work off some of the frustration he was feeling over not being able to control the circumstances surrounding his life right now.

The sun had moved across the sky by the time he had finished chopping the wood. He filled the wheelbarrow, pushed it up to the house and stacked the wood neatly beside the back door. Then he pushed the wheelbarrow back down the hill to the woodshed.

Standing at the kitchen sink, Meghan turned her head when she heard him come through the door. Her heart filled with tenderness when she saw the sadness in his eyes. She gazed at him for a moment and it was as though she was seeing him, *really* seeing him, for the first time in a long time.

He wasn't a young man anymore. She noticed the few lines that crinkled around the outer edges of his eyes and the flecks of grey in his dark hair. And when he moved, although his tall body was still lean and muscular, his broad shoulders no longer swayed with the confidence he'd shown in his younger days. And yet, she thought to herself, at 50 years old he was still a very handsome man.

She had a dinner of pot roast, mashed potatoes and gravy, and warm rolls with butter waiting for him on the kitchen table. After seating himself at the table, Meghan sat down and they bowed their heads while Rod said grace before they began to eat their meal together. Half way through the meal, Rod paused for a moment to catch Meghan's eye. "Everything's delicious, Meghan," Rod said, expressing genuine appreciation.

"I'm glad you like it," Meghan answered softly, lowering her head. It had been a long time since she'd prepared a meal like this.

After they'd finished eating, Rod went upstairs to take a shower while Meghan busied herself in the kitchen. After he stepped out of the shower he dried himself off, pulled on a pair of light grey sweatpants and a dark T-shirt, and laid down on the bed to rest.

It was dark by the time Meghan had finished putting away the leftovers and cleaning up the kitchen. With her work done, she headed upstairs and took her shower. After she dried herself off, she slipped into a pale peach nightgown and walked into the bedroom where Rod lay relaxing on the bed. Rod saw her pull the ivory hair combs that had been holding her loosely wrapped bun in place. Her thick, curly auburn hair fall onto her bare freckled shoulders and Rod was struck with the realization that it had been a long time since....

His eyes roamed over her womanly curves and he drew in a quick breath, feeling something stir within him. Meghan turned and Rod captured her with his eyes. He patted the empty place beside him and Meghan moved slowly towards him until she was standing next to the bed. Rod gently pulled her down onto the bed next to him, drawing her closer to him until she was breathing in his masculine scent. Suddenly his mouth was on hers, moving hungrily, and she circled her arms around his neck.

Neither of them had realized until this moment just how deprived they had been of the other. When his kisses became more urgent, Meghan found herself responding completely, giving in to the powerful passion that still lay there between them, beneath the layers of pain.

Chapter 15

Valdoma stood at the fence rail watching Raisa riding Magic around the inside of the outside ring. Her wavy, dark hair flowed out behind her, and her boldly printed skirt swirled in the wind as Magic cantered around the ring. Resting her hand on the fence post, a thoughtful half-smile curved Valdoma's mouth.

Raisa was so much taller now than she had been the first time she had ever laid eyes on her. Now her long, black hair fell past her shoulders. It was hard to believe that four years had passed since the morning she'd found Raisa curled up in a pile of hay in the barn. A glimmer of satisfaction filled Valdoma's eyes. Raisa was *her* daughter now. She had made sure of that by using all the strength and determination that lay within her. Sergi had not been able to stop her and she would never ever let anyone take Raisa away from her now.

Sergi came to stand beside Valdoma. He

followed Raisa with his eyes too, as she jumped off the cantering horse, and then jumped back onto him after he had made his way around the ring.

"Her form is very good," Sergi said, sounding impressed. "She should do very well for her first time under the big tent." Then his dark brows creased with worry. "We are leaving in less than a week, Valdoma. Tell me, what are we supposed to do?"

Valdoma's thoughts drifted backward in time for a moment as she remembered another conversation she and Sergi had had when he had called her from his mobile phone just a few weeks after Raisa had come to them.

He spoke excitedly. "When I was in the market, the police came. They were looking for a little girl who is lost. When I left, they were going from house to house in the village. You must give them the child, Valdoma. Just tell them the truth—that you found her in the barn."

There was a brief pause on the line as Valdoma began forming a plan in her mind.

Sergi's voice was filled with anger. "Do you hear me, Valdoma!? You must do as I say!"

She tried to sound convincing. "Don't worry, Sergi. I will take care of everything. I will talk to the police." She'd hung up the phone abruptly and turned to Baba. "Quick, Baba, take Raisa. Take her to the church and keep her inside until I come for you."

Valdoma was pleased with herself as she pulled the counterfeit passport out of one of the pockets in her skirt and handed it to Sergi. He took it and looked it over without a sound, showing no signs of approval or disapproval, before handing it back to her. Within the week, they joined the rest of the gypsy troupe at the airport, and boarded a plane headed off to distant lands.

It was early morning when they landed in Ireland. The hum of the plane's engine went silent, and the troupe made its way down to the tarmac. They gathered their luggage and then unloaded the cargo plane. Once they had everything loaded into the trailers, they travelled by road to Galway—the blustery city with its medieval cobblestone streets—and set up their circus tent in Eyre Square.

Once everyone had finished unpacking, some of the men and women took their fishing poles and went to the angler's shop to buy a pail of bait, and then headed off to the river to spend part of the afternoon fishing. Valdoma, Baba, and Rosie stayed behind with some of the other women and children to help care for the animals. When the fishermen returned a few hours later, Sergi and the other men roasted the trout they had caught over an open fire. When everyone had finished eating, one-by-one, they wandered away from the dying fire to find a place where they could rest.

In the evening, the show was about to begin. Behind the big green and white striped tent, beyond the view of the spectators, horses snorted and swished their tails while riders loosened up by jumping up and down and running in place. They mounted their horses and waited until it was time to enter the ring.

Inside, the air was heavy with the odor of exotic animals, freshly oiled leather, and hot buttered popcorn. When the other riders had finished their acts, Sergi and Valdoma took their turn in the ring while Rosie waited excitedly until it was her turn to perform. Finally, after what seemed like an eternity, the moment had arrived.

She jumped up and stood on Magic's back, and rode into the ring for her first public performance, her arms extended out to the hushed crowd. She rode around the ring, feeling the rhythm of Magic's movement beneath her bare feet. She took a breath and executed a perfect somersault, both surprised and thrilled by the sudden burst of applause that followed from the enraptured audience.

She continued around the ring, listening for the hoof beats of Arielle and Bashalde cantering up behind her. She concentrated on the rhythms of Magic's movement and the sound of the hoof beats of the horses behind her, and then vaulted backward through the air, landing with one foot on each of the other horse's backs.

She rode around the circus ring straddling the space between the two horses, listening intently for Magic's hoof beats. When she heard them behind her, she vaulted backward through the air in one fluid motion, landing squarely on his back. The breathtaking ride gradually slowed and then she somersaulted off the stallion's back and onto the ground, landing on her feet, bowing deeply before the cheering crowd.

The sound of fireworks started drifting into the tent now, and spectators hurried out to watch the dazzling display against the blue-black sky. Most of the performers and their horses had already cleared out of the tent, leaving Sergi, Valdoma, and Rosie, still feeling the warm flush of a successful performance, to remain under the tent a few minutes longer.

Sergi smiled down at Rosie. "You were fantastic. You are a natural. The crowd loved you. How does it feel to be a real circus performer?" he asked.

Rosie's face beamed as she smiled up at him, excitement dancing in her eyes.

Then Sergi's expression grew serious, his voice filling with pride. "We are Roma. The circus is our life."

After they had finished their circuit of performances in the beautiful, lush green country of Ireland, they were off to Scotland, the land of castles shrouded in mist, wild heather moorlands, and rolling grass hills.

While touring Scotland, the troupe passed the time regaling one another with outlandish tales and singing uproariously, filling the trailers with an exuberant spirit of comradeship during the long hours they spent on the road. The days went by in a flurry of activity as the circus of ornately painted wagons, exotic animals, and skilled performers stopped and set up in the towns and cities along the way. After their final performance in Scotland, they traveled the now familiar roads back to the airport and boarded a plane headed to England for their last circuit of performances before returning home.

From her window seat on the plane, Rosie took in the ever changing scenery miles below. Thick white clouds briefly gave way to reveal glimpses of the Irish Sea. When the plane eventually began its descent, she could see rocky cliffs towering over sparkling sapphire blue water. Then the land became a patchwork of naturally grazed fields until even the treetops became recognizable. Dirt roads gave way to roads that were paved. And now tall buildings appeared. Finally the airport came into view.

After the plane landed, everyone went about their familiar routine of unloading everything. Then they set off down the road towards the town where their first evening performance was to be held. Once they had arrived, the men went straight to work setting up the tents with practiced skill while the women began unpacking and preparing their noon-day meal.

Young children ran about burning off the excess energy they'd built up on the plane flight, while horses quietly nibbled the grass beneath the nearby trees. After everyone had finished eating their meal, the animals were fed theirs. Then, everyone rested until it was time to prepare for their acts.

Calliope music drifted in through the small, open windows of the trailer where Rosie was doing her warm-up exercises. She watched as two clowns passed by just outside the window and felt the excitement building inside her. This would be their last performance before they all boarded a plane the next morning for the long flight home.

Finished with her warm-ups, she stood in the doorway of the trailer, reflecting on how magical this tour had been, so much more magical than all the other tours before, because now she wasn't just watching the show from the shadows. Now, she was inside the ring, under the bright lights, just like all the other performers. Oh how she loved the circus!

She loved all of its fascinating sights and sounds, and she loved watching all the other performers. She even loved the hard hours of practice she put in for her own performance. And now, best of all, she loved being inside the ring during the show. And even though there was still a part of her that was amazed at how she had become experienced enough to perform under the bright lights, it was as though she had done this all her life. It was such a natural part of her now—of who she was. Now, if

Sergi asked her how it felt to be a real circus performer, she would say, "It just feels right. It feels like this is who I am."

As the final show was nearing its end, Sergi, Valdoma, and Rosie stood just out of view of the audience and the crowd fell into a hushed state of expectation. Then, in an instant, all the lights went out and the crowd held its collective breath.

In the darkness, the atmosphere was charged. Then an array of bright colors streamed across Valdoma. She was a vision of loveliness in her glittering indigo attire, her black hair plaited and gleaming and falling down to her waist. She danced upon Bashalde's back as he jogged gracefully around the ring. The dance was exquisite, and the awestruck crowd rose to their feet. As she rode off stage while pirouetting on the horse's back, the crowd stood, erupting with cheers and applause.

Away from the bright lights now, Valdoma heard someone call her name. As she dismounted, her eyes adjusted to the darkness and she saw that it was Rosie.

Rosie looked up to her imploringly, her eyes wide. "Teach me to dance like that... please?"

With the circus season over, Sergi, Valdoma, and

Rosie settled in for a chilly autumn that turned into a cold winter, waiting for the weather to finally turn warm again. As the days got longer, Rosie began spending more and more time outdoors. One morning, while helping Sergi make the morning rounds of caring for the animals, Sergi left Rosie and headed out to the lion's enclosure.

Rosie watched him return, carrying something in his arms. When he came near enough, he held it out to her. It was one of Simza's new cubs, less than a week old. Delight and eagerness shown in Rosie's eyes as she reached out for the small bundle of spotted fur, taking it carefully from Sergi and snuggling it close to her. She was eleven years old and she was holding a real baby lion cub!

"Simza refused to take care of her cubs," Sergi quietly explained. "The other one, the little female... she didn't make it," he said sadly.

"Don't worry Tata, I will take good care of this one," Rosie said soothingly. "What shall we call him?" she asked, stroking the little cub's soft fur.

"Well... let us think. He looks like he will be big and strong like his tata, so we'll give him something of Aurari's name. We will call this little fellow Ari," Sergi answered.

"Ari," Rosie murmured, hugging him gently.

Sergi nodded his head approvingly. "Now we will go to Valdoma and have her show you how to prepare a bottle for him. You will have to feed him every two hours. Valdoma will give him his night feedings so that you can sleep."

"Okay Tata," Rosie said happily.

Minutes later, Valdoma handed a bottle filled with formula to Rosie. She sat down carefully on the grass, the little lion cub still in her arms. As soon as she put the bottle to his mouth, he began greedily sucking until the bottle was empty. Rosie sat perfectly still and watched him as he fell asleep in her arms. Then she rose and carried him up to the house and into her room. She wrapped him in a little blanket and laid him down in the center of her bed.

In the days and weeks that followed, Rosie and Ari became inseparable. Ari slept contentedly in Rosie's bed each night. When he had grown too big for a bottle, they ate their meals together, with Ari plopping down on the floor next to where she was seated at the table, his head nearly buried in his dish, chewing noisily until every last piece of meat was gone.

On one early afternoon during his play time, two-

and-a-half-month old Ari scampered about, his curiosity leading him along until he haphazardly slipped under the horses' fence.

Rosie laughed from her seat on the grass, watching him hurry away from the approaching horses, squirming back under the fence and running back to her for safety. He climbed into her lap and settled down, purring and sucking on her fingers for comfort.

"He is quite the character, isn't he?" Sergi asked, coming up behind them. "He does not seem to know that he is the king of the beasts! One day, those horses will be running away from him," he said laughing and walking away.

"Oh Ari, you're nothing more than a big scaredy cat," Rosie said teasingly to the contented little ball of fur who continued to suck nonchalantly on her fingers.

Ari was growing quickly. At four months he was still sleeping in Rosie's bed at night, curled up with the now tattered blanket. When he wasn't sleeping with it, he liked to drag it around the yard—his make believe "prey".

When he had reached six months, they had to move him out of the house and into a cage in the lion barn. Every time Rosie came to rescue him from his confinement, he would throw himself at her, putting his huge paws on her shoulders and licking her face with his rough tongue. Then he would follow her around the yard, crouching down and playfully stalking her before slowly moving forward to pounce on her from behind. They would tumble to the ground and roll around in the thick grass until one day when Sergi announced, "No more! He's getting too big and too strong. He could hurt you without meaning to."

Chapter 16

On the evening of August 15th, the local TV station ran a segment marking the fifth anniversary of Rosie's disappearance in an effort to renew the public's interest in the unsolved case. Everyone who knew Meghan—including Rod—was surprised when she agreed to being interviewed. Meghan knew there were people who thought she should just get over it and get on with her life.

But she couldn't just "move on" or "get over it". The never ending desire to hold her child in her arms again was a constant driving force. Coupled with the maternal love she felt for her child, she was once again pushing herself far beyond her limits in a courageous effort to make a public plea for the safe return of her daughter.

Trisha Peterson, the slim young anchorwoman, sat in a plush burgundy chair that had been precisely angled towards an identical chair where Meghan, wearing a short-sleeved dark blue dress, was seated, her hands folded neatly in her lap. Meghan appeared pale and somber next to Trisha with her glowing tan and a summery fuchsia scarf draped loosely about her neck.

Halfway through the interview, Trisha paused and looked at Meghan thoughtfully. "Does it ever get any easier? Is there ever a time when a whole day goes by and you realize that it was a good day? A day without painful memories haunting you?"

Meghan answered without hesitation. "No, it only gets harder."

Trisha's eyes narrowed thoughtfully. "In what way?" she prodded.

Meghan lowered her eyes for a moment as if considering her thoughts before looking up to meet Trisha's serious blue eyes. "With each day that goes by, my hope for finding my daughter grows weaker. Time is slipping away from me… from us. When I think about all the things I've already missed—each birthday, each Christmas, each first day of school—I ache all over. I'll never get those days back."

Meghan looked back down to her hands. "There are times when I think that if I could just forget for more than a few hours, or even for a few minutes at a time, it would be a blessing…. Maybe even a relief," she said looking up and once again meeting Trisha's eyes. "But it never goes away. And the truth is that I don't ever want to forget, because if I forget her, then I will have truly lost her."

The silence that followed Meghan's statement in the news room was so complete that the air seemed to have thinned into almost non-existence. Trisha quietly ended the interview by thanking Meghan and then providing a list of contacts for anyone with any information about the missing child, phone numbers and contact information appearing on the screen below a picture of a seven-year-old Rosie. What the cameras were kind enough not to show, was Meghan, weeping and visibly shaking, being led off camera and out of the newsroom by one of the crew.

Meghan spent the rest of the week in bed struggling to hold onto what little control she had left over her fragile emotions. The interview had taken its toll on her. It had brought it all back to life and drained her of almost all of her strength. Each time she got out of bed, it was like trying to move through quicksand. She cried when Rod made the decision to call the doctor to ask him to refill her prescription again. She'd been off of the medication for over six months.

"It's just a little setback, Honey," Rod said as he sat down on the bed beside her. "You'll get through this. You just have to allow the pills to help you again, just like they did last time."

Meghan nodded slowly, unable to put up even the smallest bit of a fight. By the end of the week, and with the help of the medication, Meghan slowly began to fight her way through the urge to stay curled up in bed. Looking out her bedroom window one morning, she could see the late summer flowers starting to bloom.

Summer was almost over, and there was a world outside her door that she would somehow have to face once again. She hadn't seen Stevie for a few weeks now, and wondered how she was doing. It seemed to Meghan that she was the only friend Stevie had, and even though Stevie didn't show it, she felt that Stevie needed her. And without question, she needed Stevie.

When she reached Stevie's place, she found Stevie with a water hose in one hand, a fine mist spraying up into the air, looking as though she had turned the hose on herself a time or two as well. Meghan stood pondering the comical side of Stevie for a moment.

Stevie, with her quirky ways, was like an oasis in the midst of the dry reality that was Meghan's life. She had a unique approach to her life—like there was some kind of delightful secret hidden just below the surface, but it was just so joyous that some of it bubbled out whenever she got carried away on one of her whims. When that happened, a mischievous glint would fill her eyes as a Cheshire cat grin spread across her face.

Stevie turned to Meghan, tiny droplets of water rolling off of her garden hat, and gestured with her free hand toward the garden. "Thought I'd water everything one last time," she said reflectively. "Want to cool off?" she asked, that Cheshire cat grin making a sudden appearance as she pointed the hose in Meghan's direction.

"No thanks," Meghan answered, daring to move closer even though she wasn't quite sure what Stevie was going to do next.

After Stevie had turned the garden hose off, she headed towards the back door. "Come on in and sit a spell," she called over her shoulder, waving for Meghan to follow her inside. A huge assortment of drying herbs and flowers hung tied and bundled from every available space in the cheerful little kitchen, both windows open wide to allow the warm breeze to dry them naturally.

Stevie saw Meghan looking around her kitchen and her face brightened. "It's harvesting time," she announced happily. "I've been out cutting every morning this week just after the dew evaporates, but before the sun is high enough in the sky to rob anything of its natural oils."

Stevie and Meghan both looked at her kitchen table. It was completely covered with the different shapes and sizes of canning jars that would be used to store the harvest of herbs and flowers once they had finished drying. Several sheets of paper labels were mixed among them.

"Why don't we go into the sitting room?" Stevie offered. "We'll be more comfortable there."

After they had settled into the comfortable room, Meghan listened to Stevie's continuous friendly chatter trying her best to listen to everything she was hearing without getting distracted. When Stevie had apparently exhausted herself by filling her in on everything she'd been doing during Meghan's absence, they sat in silence for a while. Meghan settled back into her chair and gazed thoughtfully at the portrait over the mantel.

Stevie followed Meghan's gaze as if reading her thoughts, and contemplated the portrait of Myles too, her brows furrowing as she concentrated. She turned to face Meghan, her expression changing to one of complete confusion. "I can't clearly remember what happened that afternoon, but I'm sure it was all just a devil of a misunderstanding. All I know is that by the next morning, he was gone. He must have thought I was to blame, but I'd like to think he's forgiven me by now."

Meghan sat quietly in the chair and waited, wondering if any of the details of that afternoon would come back to Stevie's mind. But Stevie just stared straight ahead, her expression having gone completely blank.

The next day, Meghan decided to go for another walk to visit Stevie, looking forward to spending another afternoon with her friend. She knew she could have called to see if Stevie was home before leaving her house, but Stevie never really seemed to go anywhere. Over time, Meghan had come to realize that Stevie lived a very solitary, secluded life. She might even go so far as to describe her as a recluse, but Stevie appeared to be content and happy living her life her way.

As she approached the little grey bungalow, Meghan caught sight of Stevie towards the back of the field. She was wearing a pale turquoise blouse and a long, flowing skirt that looked like a giant watercolor with its wide, washed-out horizontal stripes of peach, turquoise, and yellow. To Meghan's sudden disappointment, she realized that Stevie had already set out on a walk of her own and was walking away from the house. It looked like she was carrying something, but they were too far apart for Meghan to make out what it was. She thought about calling out to her friend, but Stevie had already crossed over the boundary of her own property and was now crossing Baker's field. It looked like she was headed in the direction of the church up on the hill.

Meghan sighed and decided to stop by again after finishing her errands in town. Then she suddenly remembered offering to stop at the post office the next time she went into town to check on a package that was supposed to have been delivered to Stevie's house.

When Meghan walked through the door to the post office, a young man with neatly trimmed short brown hair and hazel green eyes greeted her with a pleasant smile. The nameplate on the counter in front of him read, "Harlan Foster – Postmaster".

"May I help you?" he asked, still smiling.

"I hope so," Meghan said returning a small smile. "My neighbor, Stevie Jensen, has been having some trouble with her car. It's in the garage being repaired, and her husband has been away for quite some time. She's been expecting a package that should have been delivered about a week ago, but it still hasn't arrived so I offered to stop in for her to see if it was here."

Harlan's smile quickly faded and his mouth twisted into a cynical grin. "Stevie Jensen? That eccentric old lady who lives down the hill below the church yard?"

Meghan nodded.

"Her husband's been dead for fifteen years! He's buried up in the North Road cemetery." A shadow suddenly passed over the smooth contours of his face. "Poor old Myles," he said, this time shaking his head. "He and my father were best friends. They used to go hunting together. They'd take weekend trips up north and come back with a bear or a moose in the back of the pickup every time. They were as close as brothers. Dad was one of the pallbearers at his funeral. Cried like a baby the whole time he was carrying Myles' coffin, but Dad wasn't a man who was afraid to show his emotions, not like most men.

"The police said it was an accident, but he was always saying that the police should have done a more thorough investigation of his death. They found a high level of poison in his bloodstream when they did the autopsy—high enough to be fatal—but the police said there was no evidence that she'd done it on purpose. It sure gave the local gossips something to buzz about though. A lot of people believe it wasn't an accident, and that's why she's kind of crazy... you know... because she feels guilty over what she did."

Meghan listened, dazed and unblinking, unable to form a coherent thought.

Harlan pushed a yellow slip of paper towards Meghan. "Sign here."

Meghan signed the slip of paper, picked up the package he had placed on the counter, and hurried out the door and across the parking lot to her car. On the short drive home, Harlan's words echoed in her mind. She had to find out for herself if what he'd said was true.

After pulling into the driveway and shutting the engine off, Meghan climbed out of the car, forgetting about the package sitting on the passenger seat. She headed straight for the backyard and walked down the path that led to the fields beyond. She needed some time to gather her thoughts, still struggling to make sense of Harlan's disturbing revelation. Maybe the fresh air would help clear her mind a little. Or maybe she was just too afraid to find out that what he had said about Stevie was true.

She made her way through the first field. Then she made her way through the second field—not even slowing her pace to watch the two horses grazing contentedly inside the fence rail. By the time she had crossed Baker's field, her mind had finally stopped racing. She followed the narrow foot path that led up the hill and skirted around the edge of the church yard and beyond, and stepped into the cemetery.

A sudden cool breeze sent chills up and down her spine. She walked along the uneven rows of gravestones, reading the names and dates on each one until there it was, real and solid and close enough for her to reach out and touch its cold smooth surface. The inscription on it read: Myles Orville Jensen, May 5, 1949 – July 20, 1999.

A clear glass vase filled with a bouquet of freshly picked flowers sat at the foot of the headstone. Meghan stared at the colorful flowers, suddenly sensing a presence behind her. She turned around slowly and was immediately frozen in place by Stevie's vacant stare. Her face was so pale that she looked as though she was the one who had died. Meghan was surprised when Stevie fell to her knees and started weeping into her upturned hands.

Meghan's heart filled with the sorrow she felt for Stevie, watching her friend having to face such a devastating loss and maybe even her own demons. She turned to look at the gravestone again, bowing her head to offer up a few silent prayers, hoping it would give Stevie a few moments of privacy. When there were no more sobs to be heard, she turned around to comfort her friend, but she was gone. Meghan cast one last glance at the smooth granite headstone where Myles Orville Jensen lay several feet below, and began to walk away, leaving him to rest in peace.

Chapter 17

It had been happening on and off for the past three months, and Sergi's patience had finally run out. As he came into the kitchen, he was outraged, his voice agitated as he spoke to Valdoma. "Again the lion's cage is filthy! It stinks! Have you seen Ceasar? I put him in charge of my lions, but he is not taking proper care of them! What am I paying him for?!"

Rosie spoke up out of concern for the big cats. "I saw him as he was going down behind the barn with Emilian, Tata. He had a bottle in his hand."

Irritated, Sergi turned around and stormed out of the house without uttering another word, slamming the door behind him.

That evening, Rosie could hear Sergi and Ceasar exchanging sharp words. Sergi was confronting Ceasar about spending his time drinking too much palinca, and not cleaning the lion cages, but Ceasar kept interrupting him, denying everything. Finally, Sergi's voice rose in anger above Ceasar's, booming all the way down to Rosie's bedroom.

"You no longer have a place here working for me! I am finished with your disrespect, and your lies! You must leave right now, and never return!"

Ceasar must have backed down quickly at Sergi's violent outburst because there was an immediate silence that followed, save for the sound of the back door closing with a loud clap. Rosie turned over onto her side with Sergi and Ceasar's words still echoing in her mind, but maybe now that Ceasar was no longer in charge of taking care of the lions, Sergi would hire someone who would take better care of them, and Ari would be okay. After she had repeated that last thought over and over in her mind, she was finally able to drift off to sleep. When morning came, Rosie found out what Sergi's new plan for the lion's care was.

"I am going to keep Emilian on. We will have him train the lions, but you're a big girl now. You can help me with some of the cleaning and feeding.

Rosie smiled and nodded her head, delighted that she would be able to spend more time with her affectionate, albeit sometimes rambunctious, Ari. But soon, it became clear that Ceasar was not about to let the matter rest. He had returned on two occasions, each time drunk and smelling of palinca. The potent brandy seemed to intensify his already burning anger over Sergi firing him. Now, Sergi and Ceasar were once again standing face to face in the kitchen.

Rosie had been sitting on her bed making a huge purple paper crown for Ari. He was going to be one year old on Saturday. As soon as she heard the raised voices, she opened her bedroom door and quietly walked towards the kitchen, stopping just outside the kitchen door, looking around the corner to watch what was happening,

"When are you going to pay me?" Ceasar demanded.

"I have already paid you all that I owe you!" Sergi retorted. "You don't remember because you drink too much palinca. That is not my problem!"

"No! You are trying to trick me, to steal from me!" Ceasar said angrily, pointing a finger at Sergi's chest.

"How dare you accuse me of stealing in my own house! Get out of here!" Sergi yelled indignantly.

"No!" Ceasar yelled back. "I am not leaving here without my money! I demand that you pay it to me now!"

Sergi's expression suddenly changed. "I have an idea of how we can solve this problem," he said, his voice turning deadly calm. "It is right in my gun cabinet," he said, turning and quickly striding towards the cabinet in the next room.

Rosie watched as all the color drained from Ceasar's face. As soon as Sergi's back was turned, he ran for the door, shouting on his way out. "You will be sorry you have done this to me! I will make you pay one way or another!"

Valdoma had just come up from the barn as Ceasar was running away, running across the yard like a frightened rabbit. When she entered the kitchen, Sergi was standing just inside the door, his eyes staring into the darkness behind her. Her dark eyes met his. "I just saw Ceasar. Why was he in such a hurry to leave?" she asked, and then glanced down and saw the gun in Sergi's hand. "What is going on?" she demanded.

The murderous gleam in Sergi's eyes was menacing. He gripped the gun's handle tighter, looking as though he was ready to explode. "I have told him that he no longer works for me and that he must stay away from here. I have had enough of him," he fumed.

"Sergi, put the gun away. Do not get yourself into any trouble. Ceasar is not worth it. If he comes here again, we will call the police," Valdoma said, and then added, "But if you do call them, make sure Raisa is nowhere to be seen."

Still standing in the doorway, Rosie was too frightened to come out, but she'd heard what Valdoma had said to Sergi and wondered at her words. Why would she have to hide? What would happen to her if the police did see her?

That night, Rosie tossed and turned, remembering Ceasar's words and wondering if he would return to cause more trouble. After finally falling into a restless sleep, she woke with a start, feeling as though something was wrong. She jumped out of her bed and rushed to the window, frantically pulling it open, climbing out, and then racing across the yard to the horse barn.

Inside the barn, she slowly felt her way to Magic's stall, unlatching the door. After slipping his halter on, she led him outside and jumped onto his back. She pressed her knees into his sides with such urgency that he went almost immediately into a canter. She turned him in the direction of the open field before moving him into a full gallop. At the end of the field along the edge of the woods, a huge fire burned brightly. The moon hid behind the trees as if it was afraid to witness what was about to happen.

As they got closer to the fire, Rosie heard gunshots, and immediately slowed Magic's pace. Slowly moving closer, she could now make out the scene unfolding before her. Two men were dragging something, a large animal maybe, across the dirt. When they reached the huge fire, they lifted it as high as they could and threw it—a huge carcass of tawny gold—into the flames.

Ari! A silent scream lodged in her throat. She watched the men back away from the fire, the smoky odor of burning fur and flesh filling the air, making it hard for them to breathe. Now the men were running toward her, holding their flaming torches up high. Had they seen her and Magic standing in the open field when the moon had finally risen up from behind the trees?

Tears blinded her eyes as she spun Magic around and pressed her knees into his sides. She couldn't hear Magic's hooves hitting the ground over the pounding of her heart, but maybe they weren't even hitting the ground at all. He was moving so fast it felt as though the two of them were flying. When they reached the barn, Rosie silently slid off, staring into the field behind her to see if she had been followed. The only thing staring back at her was the darkness.

She led Magic to the open paddock and walked him around the inside rail to cool him down before leading him back into the barn and into his stall. After unlatching his halter and closing the stall door, she slipped out the barn door, crouching down and scanning the perimeter of the yard before making a run for the house and the safety of her room.

When she woke the next morning, for the first few seconds she thought that it had all been a horrible dream. Then the reality of the previous night's events pressed down heavily upon her. She had the strongest urge to get out of her bed and run. She wanted to run and to keep on running until she was far away—until she was someplace where bad things didn't happen. But there was an invisible weight sitting upon her chest, and for the longest time she couldn't even lift herself up from the bed.

She could hear Sergi and Valdoma talking to one another, Valdoma moving around the kitchen making Sergi his breakfast. Sergi had called her for breakfast and chores, but she had stayed in her room pretending to be asleep so she wouldn't have to go with him. She couldn't bring herself to tell them what she had witnessed the night before. She just couldn't.

After a while, Rosie heard Sergi close the door behind him as he went out to feed the lions, and knew it wouldn't be long before he found out that Ari was missing. He'd find both Aurari and Simza waiting in their cages for him to feed them, the doors to their cages safely locked. But Ari's cage would be empty.

When Sergi came back into the house, a cold fury burned in his eyes. Valdoma looked at him uncertainly.

"What's the matter?" she asked.

"This time he has gone too far!" Sergi shouted angrily.

Valdoma cocked her head to one side. "Who?" she asked. "Who has gone too far? Sergi, what are you talking about?"

"When I went down to feed the lions, Ari was not in his cage. He is gone! Ceasar took him!"

"Gone? What do you mean, gone?" Valdoma stared at him in disbelief. But the look on Sergi's face convinced her that it was true. "How do you know Ceasar took him?" she asked.

"I know Ceasar took Ari because he closed the cage door and secured it after he took him out. He wanted to make sure I knew it was him, and that Ari did not just get out of his cage accidently." Sergi stared at Valdoma. "Of course it was Ceasar who took him! Who else would dare to go into a lion's cage and steal him unless he was one of his trainers?! Emilion knows nothing. I am going out to look for Ari and Ceasar right now!"

Inside her bedroom, Rosie pressed her hands tightly against her ears, trying to block out Sergi's ranting about Ari being missing, but she had heard every single word. Unable to bear listening to him any longer, she threw herself onto her bed and buried her face into her pillow weeping over her beloved Ari. On the floor, lay the unfinished purple crown.

There had been an absolute stillness in the house after Ari's disappearance. Nothing had changed for the better the next morning when Valdoma, needing some time to be by herself, had gone down to the horse barn to do the morning chores. Sergi had not come out of their bedroom until half the day was over. When he finally did come out, he was out the door without saying anything to anyone, and was gone for several hours, finally returning in time for the dinner Valdoma had waiting on the table.

"Where have you been?" Valdoma asked. "Your dinner is about to get cold."

"I have been out looking for Ceasar. He seems to have disappeared. But do not worry, I will find him and when I do, I will make him pay." His voice held that deadly calm that always frightened Rosie far more than any of his angry rages ever had.

For several hours each day after Ari went missing, Sergi would disappear. Rosie was sure he was out looking for Ceasar, but neither she nor Valdoma asked him about it. One night, while Ceasar was still nowhere to be found, Rosie stirred as she lay in her bed waiting to fall asleep. There was some kind of commotion down at the barn. The horses' neighing was shrill and panic stricken.

Magic! The men who had killed Ari now wanted to kill him too! Impulsively, she scrambled out of bed and went to the window. In the very next moment she had the window open and was slipping outside. In the pitch black she raced across the yard, stopping halfway to the barn, where she hid in the bushes, mustering the courage to go further. But something in the air had changed, and suddenly someone – or something – grabbed her by the arm from behind.

It was a mulo, she thought—one of the ghosts Baba had warned her about. The older woman was always telling stories of restless spirits, the terrifying creatures that had no bones and only three fingers on each hand. She had explained to Rosie how a mulo could appear at noon when they wouldn't create a shadow, but they mostly roamed about after dark. Sometimes they were vampires and they would search for the person who had caused their death and do horrible things to them.

"Never wander away from home or from any of our camps," Baba had warned her, "or the mulos might get hold of you. They might be lurking in the trees," she explained. She had grasped the charms that hung about her neck and pointed a wrinkled finger at Rosie. "Always wear one of these around your neck to ward them off. And remember to carry a hawthorn branch with you any time you must go out alone. It is the only thing that will kill a mulo," Baba had stated while nodding her head knowingly.

On nights when the wind blew, Rosie would lie in bed shivering with fear remembering Baba's words, her imagination conjuring up all sorts of evil creatures who would chase her through the village in her dreams. Tonight though, before she opened her mouth to scream, she heard Sergi's and Emilian's intoxicated voices booming across the yard as they came closer to the house. As they approached, the strong grip let go of her arm just as suddenly as it had grabbed it.

After a few minutes the horses quieted down in the barn, and the night seemed to settle down. Rosie waited until she heard the back door slam shut, then she crept back to the house and climbed in through her open bedroom window. Her heart was still pounding when she pulled the covers up tight. Something, or someone, was out there in the dark, and they had wanted to harm to her.

The next morning, while they were having their breakfast, Rosie told Valdoma that she had heard someone down at the barn late last night—leaving out the part that she had gone outside after dark when she wasn't supposed to. Instead, she suggested that it might have been a mulo. Valdoma just threw her head back and laughed as though she thought Rosie had just imagined the whole thing.

Chapter 18

"I'm worried about her, Mom," Meghan confided after relaying the shock of finding out that Myles was dead—that he'd actually been dead for years. "I went back to the post office this morning to talk to the postmaster before I took Stevie her package. I had hoped to talk to him privately, but by the time I'd made it up to the counter, there was a line of people behind me. When he asked me what I thought of my neighbor now that I'd had some time to think about what had happened to Myles, everyone just started talking about it.

"It sounds like Miles was loved and respected by everyone who knew him. He was kind and gentle and always available to help anyone who needed help. When he died so suddenly, and under such suspicious circumstances, everyone in town blamed Stevie. It sounds like they've never stopped blaming her either."

"I'm sorry to hear about your friend's troubles,

Honey. But she's made it this far. Maybe now she'll be able to come to grips with the whole situation and finally put it behind her. Unfortunately she can't change peoples' minds, but it really doesn't matter what they think. And she has you now. I'm sure you've been a great comfort to her, so try not to worry about her so much. I'm sure she'll make it through this difficult time."

After Meghan hung up the phone, she went outdoors to gather the laundry from the clothesline still thinking about Stevie. Why had Stevie talked about Myles as though he was still alive? Was it just too painful for her to completely accept the truth—or was she just plain crazy? And the last question had made her wonder—*did* Stevie really kill Myles?

The whole situation was disturbing, especially because it caused her to ponder something she'd rather not think about—that you never *really* know somebody. Still… she couldn't help feeling sorry for Stevie. After all, she, more than anyone else, knew what it was like to feel guilty over losing someone that you love—even if it wasn't your fault.

She carried the laundry inside and folded it into neat, separate piles. Just as she finished folding the last piece, Rod walked through the front door. "Have you been at the church all this time?" she asked.

Rod had been at the church with some of the other men in the congregation putting a fresh coat of paint on the sanctuary walls. He'd said he'd only be gone for a few hours, but he'd been gone much longer than that.

"Pastor Earl said he had something important to discuss with us and wanted to have a meeting after we finished," Rod explained, hedging around the reason for the meeting. "He didn't have all the information yet, and was going to have to fill us in on the rest of it after he'd made a few more phone calls. And there are still things that have to be worked out... dates and times for one thing... before we can go ahead and schedule the... uum... meetings," Rod said slowly as if he was trying to prepare her for something that would upset her.

While Rod was trying to break the news to her about what he was already planning to do in the very near future, Meghan's thoughts had already begun drifting. She was losing interest in what sounded to her like church business matters. And she was still worried about Stevie. She couldn't stop wondering if she was okay.

Rod cleared his throat as if to say something, but

Meghan started speaking as if she hadn't heard him. "I'm going to visit Stevie later this afternoon," she said, sounding as if she were simply thinking out loud. "I think she might need someone to talk to."

Rod just nodded his head slowly and headed upstairs to shower and get dressed for work. When he left, Meghan was sitting in one of the rocking chairs on the front porch. She watched him back his truck out of the driveway and start off down the road. She began rocking, and continued rocking for nearly an hour, as if preparing herself for what she was about to do next, unsure of what state of mind she might find Stevie in when she reached her place. Then, she started off slowly down the road.

Stone angels stood at the entrance of the North Road cemetery, but Meghan could barely make out their weathered forms from where she was sitting so she returned her gaze to the colorful flowers before her.

She and Stevie were sitting in willow chairs by the garden, watching two humming birds hover over a delphinium. She turned to look at Stevie, but Stevie's gaze had shifted toward the angels.

"I'd made a strong batch of foxglove tea," Stevie confessed. "Have you ever heard of it?"

"No," Meghan answered quietly.

"Well... I used to add it to the water in my flower vases. It made the cut flowers last longer, but foxglove is poisonous. It starves the brain of oxygen and can cause the heart to stop beating. I never should have put it in the water pitcher. I'd never done it before but I'd run out of vases... and it was only that one time..." she said, her thoughts wandering back to the place where those long buried memories had been kept.

"He must have just thought it was one of my herbal teas and poured himself a glass." She smiled a pain-filled smile. "He probably added sugar and sliced lemon.... Oh Myles, my poor, sweet Myles," Stevie sobbed. "I killed him. I didn't mean to... but it happened all the same."

"Of course you didn't mean to," Meghan said. "It was an accident. That's all it was, just a very unfortunate accident."

Chapter 19

Over the next few days, Rod started spending every moment he could with Meghan, as if he was still trying to make up for having been away for most of the day on Saturday. Each morning he put the water on for coffee, and when it had finished brewing, he poured them each a cup. Then he would sit with Meghan, drinking his coffee slowly, offering to sit and have a second cup with her after they'd finished their first.

One day, he put aside some of the yard work he would have normally done before leaving for work, and turned off his work cell phone so their time together wouldn't be interrupted. He fired up the grill to cook some burgers, and coaxed Meghan into bringing everything they needed to go along with their burgers outside so they could enjoy a leisurely meal together in the sun and fresh air.

For most of that day, just like almost every other day that they had spent together since Rosie had disappeared, Meghan's gaze was focused away from Rod's, her thoughts a million miles away. When she did look at him, she thought she saw a certain look in his eyes—a look that under normal circumstances would cause her to wonder what was weighing on his mind. It was a look that made her want to ask him about it because she thought there might be a little bit of sadness mixed into it.

But these were not normal circumstances. There was almost nothing normal about the circumstances surrounding their lives these days, and there hadn't been for such a long time that she'd actually forgotten what normal was supposed to feel like. So she just let those brief instances of wondering pass.

Rod, recognizing that she was once again too caught up in her own despondent thoughts to be curious about what was on his mind, couldn't find it in his heart to start the conversation and say what needed to be said. He just kept hoping that at some point she would become interested enough to ask him what was going on. But it hadn't happened yet, and it didn't seem very likely that it was going to happen. And because of that, there didn't seem to be any way to prepare her for what was about to happen in their very near future.

"Oh Rod… please don't go," Meghan begged.

But Rod stood firm. "I have to go, Meghan. Pastor Earl said that he felt very strongly that I should be one of the two men to go with him. It's only for four weeks. I can't say no. I really feel that it's very important for me to go," he finished.

Meghan's voice thickened. "But it's so far away. Something could happen…. I don't want to lose you. I can't lose you too…. I just can't."

Rod cleared his throat. "It will all be fine, Meghan. I'll be fine, and you'll be fine, too. You'll see. I'll be back before you know it," he said, trying to comfort her.

"But a whole month, Rod."

Rod's tone softened when he saw the tears brimming in Meghan's eyes. "I can call your mother and ask her if she could come out and stay with you," he offered.

Having become fully convinced of Rod's determination to make the trip with Pastor Earl, Meghan shook her head. "No. That won't be necessary," she said coolly.

"Or I could bring you to your Cousin Patty's house before I leave, and pick you up as soon as I return," he tried.

"Rod, I'm not leaving this house," Meghan said, sounding adamant.

And Rod knew she wouldn't. Even though it had been over five years, Meghan was determined to be here in case Rosie somehow found her way home.

On the morning he was scheduled to leave, Rod closed the packed suitcase, and grabbed his cell phone off the nightstand. "Well..." he started, purposely trying to keep his tone light. "That's everything."

When Meghan didn't respond, he lifted the suitcase and headed out the bedroom door. Meghan followed him out of the room and down the staircase. Standing before the front door, he set the suitcase down on the floor and held his arms open for Meghan. She reluctantly moved forward and into his arms, letting him wrap them around her.

"Remember Honey, you can call me anytime—day or night—it doesn't matter," he said, beginning to say his goodbye to her with the most reassuring words he could think of. "I won't be able to answer when we're in the air, but I'll make sure to call you with all the flight information so you'll know when I won't be able to answer." Then he released her from his embrace, rested his hands on her shoulders, and looked into her eyes. "I'll call you the first chance I get," he said. "I love you Honey, and I'll be back before you know it. I promise."

Meghan's body stiffened under the warmth of his touch as she remembered another promise he had made to her, a promise he'd made over five years ago—that he would find Rosie. "Goodbye, Rod," she said, with barely checked emotion in her voice, before turning and walking up the stairs, leaving him standing alone at the door.

On the third day after Rod left, Meghan had come to a decision. Beginning the next morning she would eat nothing. And she would drink only water. And she would continue to do this for the next two weeks. It was late afternoon and she was sitting at the kitchen table when she had decided that she would fast—and as she usually did each day—she would pray. But she kept feeling as though there was something else she needed to do. She had just finished reading her Bible. As she closed its cover, she lifted her head and gazed thoughtfully out the window past the sloping hill behind the house all the way down to the wooded area just before the field.

And right then, she knew what she needed to do.

Leaving her Bible on the table, Meghan rose up from her chair and went to the door. She stepped out into the sunlight and made her way across the yard and down the sloping hill into the forest. She roamed through the woods picking up the largest stones she could lift and carried them to a small clearing, placing them side by side on the forest floor. Continuing to gather more stones, piling one on top of another, row upon row, she built an altar.

And each morning when she woke, she made her way down into the woods, gathering twigs that were scattered among the leaves on the ground. She placed them on the altar and started a small fire in the pile of twigs. She put the incense she had brought with her into the burning twigs and knelt before the altar while sweet aromas filled the air.

Then she tilted her face upward and cried out, pouring her heart out with fervent supplication as she wept. And then she would wait. She would just wait. And then, on the day she had spent every last ounce of raw emotion within her, while she was still kneeling silently before the altar, a wind began to drift through the trees. First, it came softly, then it became stronger and stronger until it was as if she was caught up in a whirlwind and she was oblivious to everything else that was around her. Yet, somehow in the midst of the wind there was a stillness. Then the thoughts began to fill her mind. And the secret of the Lord was revealed to her.

She had built the altar upon the exact spot where she and Rosie used to sit and watch the horses grazing in the field. Now she had given that special place to the Almighty. And she had sacrificed, and she had worshipped Him there. And when she had walked away from the altar that day, it was as though she had left Rosie there with Him—had in fact given Rosie to Him there. And in return, He had given her a song.

On that day, and on each day afterward, a melody played in her heart, *Rosie in the whirlwind, Rosie in the stillness... with Him*. And though she couldn't explain it, whenever the melody rolled round and round in her heart, she felt like weeping. But they were no longer tears of sadness that filled her eyes, instead, miraculously, they were tears of joy. Meghan no longer held onto the resentment she had felt toward Rod for leaving her. She realized now that it *had* been important for him to go away—for her sake just as well as his own.

Chapter 20

With all of their work done for the evening, Sergi and Valdoma were relaxing quietly, each with a drink in hand while Rosie sat cross-legged, reading a book by the open window. Suddenly, she stopped reading and lifted her head, tilting it to one side. She could hear music playing, and what sounded like people singing. It was very faint, but she heard it, she was sure of that.

Sergi and Valdoma either didn't hear it or were ignoring it. Rosie could tell it wasn't the music of the Romani. It was very different. She began to ask Valdoma what kind of music it was, but seeing the expression of disapproval on Valdoma's face, she thought better of it and returned to her book, secretly straining to hear the unfamiliar music.

Deep inside the barn, Magic's ears pricked forward and his nostrils flared. Then he lifted his head and whinnied.

Rosie got up quickly and ran to the back door,

ready to run down the slight slope of the hill behind the house to the barn, but Valdoma had followed her into the kitchen.

"Where do you think you are going?" Valdoma asked her.

"Magic... I can hear him. He's restless—" Rosie began.

"Raisa, you know you are not to go out when it is this much past dinner time," she admonished. "You do not have to worry about Magic. He is safe."

"But Ceasar..." Rosie tried again.

"Will not ever come here again. He will not ever harm Magic or any of the other animals. You can rest assured that Sergi took care of that," she said darkly. "Now go and finish with your reading. Everything is fine," she said, ushering Rosie back into the living room and shutting the window.

The next night, coming from somewhere out in the darkness, Rosie could hear the music playing again. She sat up in her bed and listened to the people singing.

Then she heard Magic whinny from inside the barn. She climbed out of bed and went to her window. Just outside the window, all of Baba's whispered warnings seemed to rise up in the night air, waiting to grab her and immobilize her in their fearful grip. But Magic's insistent whinny called to her again, so she quickly climbed out the window and raced across the yard, thinking only of him until she was finally pulling the barn door shut behind her, leaning against it for just a moment to catch her breath.

In their stalls, the other horses shifted nervously from side to side. With her heart pounding and her hands trembling, Rosie unlatched Magic's stall door and let him follow her out the backdoor of the barn into the open air.

In her bedroom, Valdoma stirred and struggled to awaken. "Raisa..." she murmured as she tried to get out of bed, but the room was spinning and it felt as though she was too heavy to lift herself up—her mind, body, and soul completely wrapped up in the warm cocoon that came from drinking too much palinca.

Rosie grasped Magic's mane with one hand and swung herself up onto his back and together they spirited off into the night. Together, they followed the sound of the music until Magic eventually slowed before coming to a complete stop.

Not more than a hundred yards in front of them

was a huge canvas tent. Rosie slid from Magic's satiny back and moved closer. It didn't look like the circus tents she had grown used to seeing. Although this one was also very big, there were large graceful gold letters stretching above the entrance. Rosie sounded out the word in her mind—*REVIVAL*.

She could easily make out the silhouettes of the villagers gathered beneath it, for it was a cloudless night with a full moon shining brightly over the open field. Lanterns hung inside the tent filling it with a warm glow. All of the other sounds of the night faded away as she drew closer to the music and the singing.

Magic waited patiently as Rosie drew closer still, and then stepped into the tent, joining the villagers. They were still singing, and some of them were clapping their hands together in rhythm to the music while they sang. Some people were even dancing.

Three men were standing in the center of a raised wooden platform lifting their hands above their heads, as if they were surrendering themselves to something, or to someone, they couldn't see. Memories from long ago slowly began to drift through Rosie's mind.

While the Holy Spirit was having its way, the

music and the singing slowly came to an end and one of the men standing on the platform began to weep. He had a faraway look in his eyes as he faced the crowd. "I have a daughter..." he began. "Her name is Rosie, and she's been missing for a long time now, but her mother and I have never stopped searching for her... have never stopped hoping...." He paused to regain his composure, his expression changing from sadness to determination. "And we will never give up. We will never stop searching for our little girl."

Rosie watched as his features softened again and deep sorrow filled his eyes.

"I'd just like to hold her in my arms again," he said, his voice wistful. Gradually, everything began to make sense to Rosie and she began to make her way up the rustic aisle, seeing his face more clearly as she drew closer to the platform.

For the briefest moment, the circus—with all its enticing splendor appeared before Rosie like a wavering vapor, and then it disappeared completely. And now, all she could see before her was her father—his eyes filling with wonder as he stared at the girl continuing to make her way down the aisle toward the platform.

Rosie moved steadily forward and stepped up onto the platform, until she was standing in front of him. She gazed into his eyes, seeing all the love and tenderness that had been waiting there for her and fell into his open arms.

Rod pulled her close, hugging her tightly, as shouts of joy and uproarious cheers erupted from the crowd. Music once again filled the air as Rosie turned to gaze out beyond the jubilant crowd.

Just beyond the huge canvas tent, the blue roan tossed his head wildly and snorted. Rosie watched him, from inside the circle of her father's arms, turn and gallop away into the darkness of night, ethereal and enchanting, beneath the gypsy moon.

Made in the USA
Lexington, KY
27 March 2017